RAW GUILT

Deborah Rine

ISBN-13: 978-1502724816 (CreateSpace-Assigned)
ISBN-10: 1502724812

For my children -

Marie-Juliette, Charles and Christopher

A continual source of Joy

Other books by Deborah Rine

Banner Bluff Mysteries:

THE LAKE

FACE BLIND

Deborah Rine can be contacted at:

www.deborah-rine-author.com

http://dcrine.blogspot.com/

Face book and Twitter

Acknowledgements

Thank you to Diane Piron-Gelman, my editor, who continues to instruct me in the art of writing.

Thank you to Denise N. Manthey, LMFT who discussed the art of psychotherapy.

Thank you to Rev. Sarah Odderstol who provided a golden gem to facing life's tragedies.

Thank you to Jan and Ken Troemel, neighbors and knowledgeable boat people.

Thank you to Anne Taylor and Lindy Trigg, readers extraordinaire.

Thank you to Google who transported me to Key West every day when it was -17° here in Chicagoland.

Thank you to my husband Larry for his positive encouragement and help in producing this book.

Raw Guilt

"C'est tellement mystérieux, le pays des larmes."
"It's such a mysterious place, the land of tears."
—Antoine de St. Exupéry, *Le Petit Prince*

PART ONE—TRAGEDY

"There's no tragedy in life like the death of a child."
—Dwight D. Eisenhower

Chapter 1 Kate

It started snowing before noon that Friday. The weather experts were caught off guard. They'd predicted six to eight inches for the Chicago area but when the storm tapered off Saturday afternoon nearly two feet of snow had fallen.

Sam called Kate at three-thirty on Friday.

"Hey, it's me," he said.

"Hi!" Her voice was flat. "When will you be home?"

"That's the thing. They've cancelled all flights coming into Chicago for the next eighteen hours." He paused and she started chewing on a thumbnail. "Kat, are you there?

"Yeah, I'm here. It's just that I've been alone with the kids and…"

"Listen, Kat—"

"Don't call me Kat. You know I don't like it."

"Sorry, babe. I'm just thinking that I might as well just go from here to Texas." He waited for a response and then continued. "I've got to be in Dallas Monday morning. I was going to fly out on Sunday night anyway."

She felt both angry and relieved. "So you won't be coming home at all?" There was a moment of silence. "Sam, I've been alone with the kids for nearly two weeks. Last Sunday you weren't even here…"

His annoyance was almost palpable from three thousand miles away.

"When will you be home from Texas?" she asked.

"Probably not until Thursday night…I know you're a bit strung out…"

Kate rarely got aggressive with Sam. He always won any argument but she felt safe with him so far away. "Strung

4

out? I'm going stir crazy. You are *never, ever* home to help out!" she shouted at the phone.

"Kat, are you drinking?" He spoke in carefully measured tones, his voice threatening. She wasn't supposed to raise her voice with him.

She didn't answer. "What's the temperature in L.A., anyway?"

"It's about eighty right now. I'm actually sitting on the balcony of my room. I'm going to go down for a swim after I talk to you."

She thought she heard murmuring in the background. "Who's there?"

"Daniella Pojoli. She's stuck here, too."

"And she's in your room, on your balcony?" She could feel the anger rising.

"Kat, calm down. Daniella just came in to get her copy of the Progeny account. You know she's working on that with me."

Sam worked for the Carepath grocery chain. He had accounts all over the country and Daniella often seemed to be on the same travel schedule. He would let her name drop when he talked about a meeting or a dinner in Minneapolis or Atlanta. He didn't keep their relationship a secret.

Kate had met Daniella at a couple of Christmas parties. Just last month she'd seen her at the awards ceremony in downtown Chicago. When Sam stepped up to the podium to receive his sales award, he had not looked at Kate; but somewhere towards the tables to the left. Kate had seen Daniella sitting there applauding, her eyes shining. She was a willowy blond with a perfect body. Kate was sure she'd had breast enhancement surgery.

Were they having an affair? On the one hand Kate felt annoyed that Sam was fooling around while she dutifully took care of hearth and home. On the other hand, it came as a relief that he was mauling some other woman.

Sam sounded irritated. "Are you there? Kat? Next weekend I'll take the kids all day Saturday and you can go to the spa and do the works. Take a whole day for yourself. Okay?"

She didn't answer. She felt like a lame dog chained to a fence and Sam was throwing her a bone.

"I've got to go now. We'll talk soon." And he hung up just like that.

He *had* to go? Where? Down to the pool with Daniella? Kate didn't even try to call back. She got up from the kitchen chair and surveyed the mess left from lunch. There was macaroni and cheese on the floor under Betsy's high chair. Five-year-old Timmy had eaten a wee bit more neatly but he had spilled some chocolate milk. The blue plastic cup lay on its side in a dirty brown pool. The sink was piled with pans from last night's supper and yesterday's lunch. The dishwasher was filled with unwashed dishes. She looked at it all and felt exhausted.

Betsy came into the kitchen. Her strawberry-blond hair stood on end and her little face was covered with blue and green magic marker. Kate looked down and saw the wet stain spreading down her daughter's pants leg.

"Betsy, did you have an accident?"

Betsy nodded. "Timmy's fault." She was frowning. "No, no, no, Timmy." She shook her finger.

"Betsy, it's not Timmy's fault or Betsy's fault. It was just an accident. Let's go change your clothes."

Upstairs Kate laid Betsy on the changing table. At nearly three years old the little girl just fit on the padded surface. She took off Betsy's wet clothes and wiped her down. Betsy looked up at her, giggling, and Kate bent down and blew bubbles on her soft, round tummy. This brought on peals of laughter.

"I love you, Betsy-boo," Kate crooned.

"Love you, Mommy," Betsy responded, her smile angelic.

This had been the third accident today. Kate decided to cheat for the rest of the day. She helped Betsy put on a pull-up diaper. The heck with potty-training! She looked in the drawer for another pair of corduroy pants or some tights but the drawer was empty. She needed to do a load of wash. Things were getting desperate. In the bottom drawer she found the white sweater her mother had knitted with little yellow ducks appliquéd across the chest. She pulled the sweater over Betsy's head and got down on the floor to put on her socks.

"Mommy, play outside."

"No, sweetheart, it's cold and snowy. Not today."

"Play in snow, Mommy." Her eyes pleaded with Kate's.

"Not today," Kate said firmly, looking into Betsy's green eyes that were so like her own.

As Kate picked up clothes off the floor and emptied the hamper, Betsy began to play with her baby doll and seemed to have forgotten about the snow. Kate went downstairs to the basement and put a load in the washer. She peeked in the family room. Timmy was lying on his tummy running his cars along a wooden track.

"Hi, Timmy!"

"Hi, Mommy." He couldn't be bothered to look up. He was way too busy. He had an unbelievable power of concentration.

Kate went back upstairs to start cleaning up the kitchen. She reached under the sink and pulled out the bottle of chardonnay. It was nearly four o'clock and already five in New York; not too early for a glass of wine.

Chapter 2   Cici

Snowplows had been hard at work around Lakeland High School, clearing the roads so that the school buses could get through. But that was at two-thirty before the three o'clock dismissal. By five o'clock when Cécile Arnaud went out to the parking lot to get into her car, the snow completely covered the roads. The parking lot was a Siberian landscape. Drifting snow had made crystalline dunes. Only five cars dotted the lot, looking like giant marshmallows in a world of powdered sugar.

Cécile wasn't afraid to drive in snow. She had grown up in Chicago and knew all about its two seasons: cold, cold winter and hot, hot summer. When she was sixteen, Oscar had taken her out to practice driving on icy roads so that she'd know how to handle the car come what may.

This afternoon Cici had stayed late because she'd received a summons from her majesty Myra Wilkins, principal of Lakeland High School. Cici had received the yellow slip at noon when she was in full swing teaching *Romeo and Juliet* to the freshman honors class. When the messenger came in to hand her the slip, the kids started to giggle. The girl had orange and purple hair in a kind of Mohawk. She wore an orange sweater and purple leggings with orange Keds. She was something else.

"I love your outfit," Cici said to the girl. "Your clothes make a real statement."

The teenager beamed and took a bow. She definitely wanted to be noticed. The class applauded while Cici peeked at the message. The rest of that afternoon she felt slightly uneasy. It was February and too early to get an official pink slip to tell her she was riffed. That usually occurred in March. What could Myra want to discuss with her? Her mind filtered

8

through the last few weeks of school. She couldn't think of any major transgressions. She had sent Rocco down to the Dean for coming in late for the third time…but that was school policy.

At three o'clock, Jeremy texted her from over in the Social Studies Department. A bunch of the younger teachers were going to a bar in the next town over for a TGIF "curriculum meeting." *R U ready to go?* the message said.

Quickly, she tapped out, *Got meeting with Myra at 4. U go ahead.*

OK c u there. Jeremy texted back.

He wasn't really a boyfriend but they hung out a lot together. On Sundays they both liked to lug their papers and laptops to Starbuck's where they graded papers and planned the next week's classes. It was a comfortable relationship. In some ways Jeremy was a little too radical for Cici. He'd marched against the war in Afghanistan and rallied for gay rights. He wrote letters to his congressmen pleading for housing for the homeless and passed out pamphlets demanding better treatment of seals. She admired Jeremy but she couldn't get riled up for all these causes. She knew it was important to make a statement, to believe in something, but she would rather spend her precious free time watching Netflix, reading or cooking.

Cici was surprised they weren't cancelling the TGIF "meeting" with this weather. While she waited for her looming rendezvous, she answered emails from parents, entered some quiz grades on the computer and began to pack up her briefcase with work for the weekend.

At four o'clock on the dot, she was waiting outside Myra's office. Lillian, the secretary, asked her to be seated. Dr. Wilkins would be with her in a few minutes. A few minutes turned into nearly half an hour. Outside the wind buffeted the building and the cold seeped through the windows across the room. Cici was thinking she could have stayed upstairs and corrected some essays while she waited. But Myra was the Queen and Cici Arnaud was her minion.

The door opened and there was Myra. She had on a black suit with a short pencil skirt and a form-fitting jacket. A lacy red top barely concealed her cleavage. She wore stiletto heels with small black bows at the toe. She was a beautiful woman of maybe forty-five or fifty and she always dressed to kill. In the hallway the boys followed her with their eyes and Cici had heard them call her a cougar.

Myra Wilkins surrounded herself with a coterie of men. The department chairs, the assistant principals; they all were men. Myra didn't relate well to other women; sharing recipes or talking hairdressers was not for her. With men it was all business - with a heavy, sensuous overtone. Myra always maintained the upper hand. They scraped and bowed and followed her like puppy dogs.

"Please come in, Cécile, sorry to keep you waiting." Myra's smile did not reach her eyes. She gestured impatiently for Cici to come into her office.

After they were both seated at the conference table, she slid a pink copy of a riffing notification toward Cici. There was no preamble. "I'm sorry Cécile, but this will be your last year at Lakeland. Student enrollment is down and we were told by the Board of Education to decrease our teaching staff. Unfortunately, you are the newest member of the English Department and you're not tenured."

"What about Ben Rogers?" Cici blurted out. "He came in three years ago, same as I did."

"Yes, but Harry made this decision. I have to stand by it."

Harry Staples was the English Department Chair. He loved Ben, who had gone to Southern Illinois, Harry's alma mater. They were often closeted in Harry's office talking together. Harry spoke with a contrived English accent and used a ten-dollar word where a simple, clear expression would do. He wore bow ties, tweed jackets with patched sleeves, and loose-fitting flannel pants, as if he were a professor at Oxford instead of a teacher at Lakeland High. Cici disagreed with a lot of his teaching methods but she thought she had successfully kept her views to herself.

"But Dr. Wilkins, this morning at the honors breakfast, the students voted me their favorite teacher. Doesn't it matter if I relate well to students?" She knew Ben had had run-ins with students and parents alike.

"I think you are a good teacher, Cécile. But the decision has been made. I am willing to write you a glowing recommendation. You can count on it."

Cici didn't give up easily. "What about Mark Chester? Isn't he retiring? Won't there be a spot for me?"

Myra Wilkins stood up and smiled coolly. "I can see you're upset. But we have made our decision. It's Friday and you'll have the weekend to digest the news." She looked out the window. "Look at that snow. We better get out of here before we're snowed in for the weekend."

Cici nodded dully. She stood up and walked woodenly towards the door, her mind a blank.

Chapter 3   Kate

The kitchen was in order. The dishwasher was gurgling. One load of laundry was in the dryer and another in the washer. Kate felt victorious. She went downstairs to the family room. Toys carpeted the floor. She cajoled the kids to help her put away the Legos, the trucks and the dolls. She made a game of it and soon the family room looked presentable.

"We did a good job, didn't we, Mommy? Can we watch a show now?" Timmy asked.

"Yes, you guys are great." She bent down and hugged them both. Then she kissed their sweet, sticky cheeks. "You can watch TV until dinner. Okay? Then we'll take a bath and read a Mrs. Piggle-Wiggle story."

Timmy loved Mrs. Piggle-Wiggle. Kate turned on the TV and switched the channel to PBS and *Sesame Street*. "Betsy, I want you to stay down here with Timmy, Okay?"

Betsy nodded happily. Her baby doll was tucked under her arm. She sat down on the old red sofa, cuddling next to Timmy. Her blankie was on her lap and she stuck her thumb into her mouth. Timmy was already mesmerized by the show. Kate thought they looked so cute together. She bent down and kissed them again.

To be on the safe side, she put up the collapsible fence at the bottom of the stairs. Then she went up to the kitchen to turn on the oven. They would have chicken nuggets, sweet potato fries and broccoli for dinner. It was almost an hour until dinnertime, so she put on the timer to remind herself to put the chicken and fries in the oven. She poured some more wine into her empty glass and added a couple of ice cubes.

Outside the kitchen window the wind slammed into the house. Blowing snow formed an impenetrable curtain. The next door neighbor's house to the south was invisible. Kate and Sam lived on a corner at 720 Ridge Road. Running along the north side of the house was Lakeland Road. It ran on an incline up to Ridge. Kate had not wanted to live on a corner but they got a great deal on the house. Immediately after moving in they put up a fence around the back yard and planted some bushes for privacy. Timmy was just a baby then.

Traffic whizzed by on Ridge all day long. Lakeland was pretty quiet except in the morning and afternoon when kids were going to and from Lakeland High. The school was five blocks away on the other side of the train tracks.

Kate walked into the living room and looked out at the street. It was dark now and the street lamp glowed in the blowing snow. On Ridge a snowdrift had formed across the intersection. It was a winter wonderland. As long as they were safe inside, she could appreciate the beauty of the storm.

She went upstairs to the room she used as a study. As she waited for her computer to boot up, she took a long sip of wine. Who cared if Sam came home or not? She got lonely sometimes, but when Sam was home she lived on tenterhooks through long days of tense silence filled with his disapproval. He told her she was a lousy housewife and a lousy mother. Since Timmy was born, Kate had gained twenty pounds and Sam was constantly on her to lose weight. He was rough and demanding with the children, who tried desperately to please him…just as she did.

Then at night he would crush her in bed, covering her mouth with his hand so she wouldn't cry out as he plunged into her again and again. Why had she married him? Kate knew the answer. It was to please her father. Butch Gifford had loved Sam like a son.

All this introspection made her depressed. Better to forget. She opened up her email and responded to a couple of friends. Sharon, her best friend from home, wanted to hear about the snow. The storm would be moving on to Indiana where Sharon lived. They always joked that Sharon got all of Kate's shit, just one day later.

Next, Kate logged on to the matchmaking site where she usually met Chet. They talked at night when the kids were asleep. He lived down in Key West and had a fishing boat. He'd sent her pictures of the boat and one of himself at the helm. She wondered if it was recent. The picture she'd sent him dated from before Timmy was born.

He usually told her about his day, the weather and goings-on in the harbor. She knew the names of some of the guys he hung out with. He seemed truly interested in her kids although he had never met them and she had never sent their picture. He had a little boy he talked about, named Carson, who was a little older than her kids. She and Chet seemed to need each other as reciprocal sounding boards. He told her he was divorced. His wife had left them several years earlier. He said he got lonely and needed to share his feelings with someone. He seemed open and sensitive…the exact opposite of Sam. Then again, this was an online friendship. Who knew if he was being totally honest?

Kate had never told anyone about this relationship. Actually, she felt kind of guilty about it. By nature she wasn't a sneaky person. But every night when Sam was out of town, she felt drawn to the computer and an hour of conversation with Chet.

She typed in: "Hey, are you there? Just thought I'd say hi. We've got an amazing snowstorm here. I bet it's eighty degrees and sunny down there. We'll talk later."

There was no response. It was too early.

She clicked into her Corel software program. She had always loved sketching and drawing. In high school her watercolors were often on display in the halls. When she got this new laptop she taught herself how to design on the

14

computer, which brought a whole new dimension to her art. Excited, she'd discussed with Sam the idea of making a career of her designs. Sam scoffed and told her it was pointless.

"Graphic design? That's a career that leads absolutely nowhere. Let's face it, you have minimal talent, and besides I want you to take care of the kids and our house." He had been irritated the rest of the evening. She had never mentioned it again.

Nevertheless, when she had a little free time she worked on decorative patterns; designs of small intricate flowers or the repetition of iconic symbols. She had a good sense of color and her compositions were striking. Lately she'd been working with shades of purple, lavender, pink and a delicate violet, with strong black lines. Purple and its sister colors were rich in variety. After all, purple was made up of red and blue, two colors that evoked entirely different moods. Together, the variety of tones was limitless.

She'd just started reworking a series of bonnets and curling ribbons when she heard the timer go off downstairs. Damn. There was never enough time to work on her designs. She sighed in frustration as she stood up quickly sending the chair careening across the wooden floor. Why did she feel on edge? She told herself to calm down. It would only take a minute to go down to the kitchen and put in the chicken nuggets and fries. Then she could come back up to finish her work. As she went downstairs, the wind slammed against the house. She heard a sharp bang; that shutter on the dining-room window must have come loose again.

Chapter 4   Cici

After her meeting with Myra, Cici walked down the hall to the
stairwell. She walked up the stairs, putting each foot squarely
on the next step. The school building was silent. All the staff
and students had left for the day. On the second floor she
walked down to the English Department office. The large
room was empty. She sat down at her desk and surveyed the
office. She didn't feel like crying. She just felt empty.

On every desk were stacks of books and papers, all of
them covered with words; pages and pages of written words.
What was the point of them all? She had always loved reading
and writing. But those words were only reporting life. They
weren't real. They weren't living and breathing. Maybe she
needed to get out and experience life instead of reading about
it. Maybe being an English teacher was not for her after all.
Apparently, Harry and Myra didn't think she had what it took.

She looked over at the disorder on Ben's desk. Ben,
who had stolen her idea for the sophomore writing project and
presented it as his own. What about him? Did he have what it
took? He spent a major part of his time coaching basketball.
He was down in the gym office more than he was up here.

Then it hit her, like a lightning bolt going off in her
brain. They *needed* Ben because of *basketball*. Everyone
raved about how well the team was doing this year. Ben was
essential to Lakeland High School. Cici didn't coach. She
wasn't essential. That was the real reason she'd been riffed.

Suddenly angry, she jumped up, pulled on her coat and
grabbed her briefcase. She needed to get out of here and go
home. She raced down the stairs, wanting to escape the school
and her own inadequacies. Pulling open the side door to the
parking lot, she was hit by a wind so strong it nearly toppled

her over. A tornado of heavy snow swirled across the parking lot forming foot high drifts and she wasn't wearing boots. Oh well! She trudged across the lot towards her car, slipping and sliding as she went.

At the car, she pulled open the driver side door and threw in her briefcase and purse. The car keys were in her pocket. She shoved them in the ignition and started the engine. Her gloves and knit hat lay on the passenger seat and she pulled them on. Behind the seat was a scraper with a brush attachment. She grabbed it, stepped outside and started sweeping the snow off the windows and headlights. She would be out of here in no time.

Chapter 5 Betsy

Betsy wanted to go outside in the snow. She wanted to make a snow angel like Mommy showed her. She nudged Timmy. He was watching TV with his mouth open.

"Go outside, Timmy? Snow?"

He didn't answer her. He was too busy watching TV. She patted him on the arm. "Go outside, Timmy?"

"Betsy, stop it, leave me alone." He pushed her away. He was watching *Curious George*, his favorite program.

Betsy got down off the sofa and dropped her blankie on the floor. She toddled into the bathroom and picked up the wooden stool she used to reach the sink when she washed her hands. It was heavy and she fell down. Boom! But she didn't cry. She got up and dragged the stool over to the fence Mommy had put up. She climbed on the stool and reached over to the banister leading upstairs. Holding on tight, she pulled herself up and stepped on the fence. It fell down on the carpet. She fell down too, on the tile floor at the foot of the stairs. Boom! Betsy looked back at Timmy but he didn't turn around.

She went up the stairs on all fours. Mommy wasn't in the kitchen. Betsy went out to the mudroom and looked for her boots. They weren't there. Only Timmy's boots were lying on the floor. She sat on the mat and pulled on his boots. They were big. She reached up for her coat. Mommy always said to put her coat on but she couldn't reach it. On the wooden seat was her bunny hat and mittens. She put them on.

Betsy reached up to turn the round knob on the back door. It wouldn't turn. She tried twisting it but her mittens slipped. She turned around and tramped through the kitchen, the dining room and into the front hall. Mommy wasn't anywhere.

Betsy reached up and grabbed the handle of the front door. It wasn't round and she could grasp it. She pulled the handle down and opened the door. Wind and snow swirled around her. She tried to step back but she tripped on the boots and fell forward. The door slammed behind her.

Outside it was cold, very cold. She wanted to go back inside, but the door was shut. She pushed herself up and banged on the door with her mittened hands but Mommy didn't hear her. Where was Mommy? She started to cry. It was too cold to play outside. She turned towards the steps and tripped, then slid all the way down on her bottom. Her legs were freezing. For a while she sat there crying. "Mommy, I cold. Mommy, come inside."

Across the street lived Mrs. Hopkins. She was a nice lady and Betsy could see the lights twinkling in the windows of her house. She saw Mrs. Hopkins moving around in her nice, warm kitchen. Betsy pulled herself up and started trudging through the snow to Mrs. Hopkins's house. Timmy's boots were too big and she fell down several times. The snow got into the boots and made her feet cold.

In the middle of the street, Betsy sat down and took off Timmy's boots to shake out the snow. She looked up and saw bright lights coming up the hill. Somebody would see her and take her home. She bent down to put the boots back on.

Chapter 6   Cici

Finally Cici had swept most of the snow off the car. She got in
and buckled her seat belt. Her feet were freezing. She turned
up the heater to high. The radio was blasting a current Katy
Perry song. She'd had the volume turned up when she drove to
work that morning. She'd been on a high, feeling great about
life and the weekend to come. Now she was plunged into a
dark, depressive mood. Life was so unpredictable. She wanted
a secure, dependable existence but instead her world had been
turned upside down.

Her knit cap and wool mittens were covered with snow.
She took them off and tossed them in the back. She needed to
calm down before she started driving in this mess but she could
still feel anger bubbling under the surface. Damn Ben, damn
Myra, and damn Harry! Cici pressed down on the accelerator.
The car shot forward and then lost traction, sliding across the
parking lot and into the curb. She put the car in reverse and
felt the wheels spin. With consistent, slow acceleration she
backed up. Then, cautiously, she turned onto Lakeland. She
could feel the road was icy under the snow, so she drove
slowly. The school building was barely visible on her right.
Two blocks further on, the road sloped down to the underpass
that ran under the train tracks. Cici felt the wheels spin as she
emerged from the underpass, heading up to the light on Eastern
Road. She slowed down even more. As the windshield wipers
beat a steady rhythm, she tapped her fingers on the steering
wheel.

Her normal route was up to Ridge and then south on
Ridge to Green Tree. Maybe she should avoid the slope up to
Ridge. She could turn left here on Eastern but she was in the
wrong lane, and another car had pulled up in the left turn lane.

20

She had four-wheel drive, so she would probably be all right. As the light turned green she proceeded across the intersection and began her two-block ascent to Ridge Road, keeping a steady speed as she plowed ahead.

Approaching Ridge, she saw what looked like a snowdrift across the intersection. It was so hard to see with the snow blowing horizontally. Her windshield wipers couldn't keep up. She decided to plow her way through. Pressing the accelerator, Cécile drove forward, gripping the steering wheel tightly.

Beneath the tires, she felt resistance. She pressed harder on the accelerator and felt a jolt, as though she had run over something. Should she back up or press forward? It could be something that would damage the undercarriage. It hadn't felt solid like metal. God, maybe she'd hit a dog. No one was around...only a furious wind and swirling snow. She put the car in park and pushed the hazard button. The red lights flashed rhythmically. She got out of the car, stepping into a snowdrift. Holding on to the hood, she moved around to the front of the car and bent down. Something was there, under the front bumper. Wishing she'd grabbed her mittens, she pushed the snow aside bare-handed.

Oh, my God. It was a child wedged under the car. A little girl. Bare legs splayed at a weird angle, her back bent, her head pushed down. In front of her lay some blue boots.

Cici moaned. What had she done? Oh, God! She got on her knees and pawed frantically at the snow. She reached under to try pulling on the child's arms, but then thought better of it. The little body was firmly wedged beneath the vehicle. Could she release the child by backing up? Would that cause more harm? Later she would wonder why she hadn't fallen apart right there.

The engine was still running. Cici went back around to the car door and pulled it open. She turned off the engine.

21

Then with shaking hands she opened her purse, pulled out her cellphone and dialed 9-1-1. In the overhead light her reddened hands resembled bloody claws.

"Help, I ran over a little child," she blurted when the dispatcher answered.

"Ma'am, where are you?"

"I don't know." She couldn't think for a moment. "Wait, yes, I'm at the corner of Ridge and Lakeland. Hurry. Please hurry."

"What is your name?"

"Cécile Arnaud."

"Could you please spell that?"

The question made no sense to her. "Are they coming?"

"Yes, calm down. An ambulance and the police should be there soon."

"I need to go back outside now. Tell them to hurry. Please." She tossed the phone onto the seat.

Outside she stumbled around to the front of the car. She lay down in the snow and reached for one of the small, cold hands.

"They're coming honey. We'll get you out. It'll be all right."

Chapter 7   Kate

In the kitchen, Kate took the package of chicken nuggets out of the freezer and placed the nuggets on a cookie sheet. On another sheet she arranged frozen sweet potato wedges. After putting the pans in the oven, she set the timer again. Then she walked over to the stairwell that led down to the family room and listened. She could hear the familiar strains of the *Curious George* program, but no other sounds. The kids must be glued to the show.

Reassured, Kate went back upstairs to finish her project. A few minutes later she heard sirens approaching. Looking out the window, she saw flashing lights. An ambulance and a fire engine were converging on their corner. There must have been an accident, but she could only make out one car. The lights kept flashing from all the emergency vehicles: red and blue, red and blue, red and blue.

Red and blue make purple. That's what she would remember thinking months later.

PART 2—ANGUISH

"That was the day my whole world went black. Air looked black. Sun looked black. I laid up in bed and stared at the black walls of my house….Took three months before I even looked out the window, see the world still there. I was surprised to see the world didn't stop."

—<u>Kathryn Stockett</u>, <u>*The Help*</u>

1 year later

Chapter 8   Kate
January, now

It was hot outside. Kate wore a black tank top and a pair of black capris. Her shoulder bones protruded from the shirt and the pants hung low on her hips. She hadn't even thought of bringing a sweatshirt but the shrink's office was freezing. She hated air conditioning and they blasted it in this building. She didn't ever want to be cold again.

She opened the office door and stood on the threshold. She could still turn back. No one was making her come here. She had more than butterflies in her stomach. More like gargantuan moths.

After a moment's hesitation she walked into the waiting room. Dr. Leah Zuckerman had an attractive office, a beige and cream-colored room furnished with a buttery-soft leather sofa and two matching chairs. On the walls were black and white prints of local scenes on Duval Street, the Hemingway home on Whitehead Street and several photos of typical Key West cottages. The general feeling was both comfortable and chic.

No one else was there. She sat down on one of the armchairs. There was no receptionist. It seemed Dr. Zuckerman did her own welcoming and clerical work. Across the room was a closed door. Did patients enter and exit by the same door? Key West wasn't that big a place if you only counted the natives. Privacy could be an issue. Maybe there was another door that led out of the doctor's office into the hallway.

Kate wasn't a native, exactly. More of a new-long-term resident. At night when the nightmares grew too much to bear, she thought about trying Texas or even California. Could she flee her monsters by moving again? Probably not. That was why she'd come to see Dr. Zuckerman: to lighten her load, to bury her grief, to feel alive. Because she was dead, dead, dead inside.

Kate reached up and felt for the locket around her neck. It was hanging inside her tank top. Then she clasped her hands in her lap and sat with her ankles crossed. It was hard to forget the rules of etiquette that had been drilled into her as a child. "Katherine, sit still. Don't fidget. Sit up straight. Don't round your shoulders. Cross your ankles like a lady." Being the only child of a strict mother and demanding father had taught her how to toe the line. She'd been the dutiful daughter they wanted.

She shivered from the cold. The inner office door opened with a whoosh. A teenaged boy came out. He glanced her way and then down at the floor as he made his way to the exit.

A moment later a woman appeared in the doorway. She was tall and slim, dressed in a cream-colored blouse and black pants. A loose bun of shiny dark hair lay at the nape of her neck. Small gold balls adorned her ears, and she wore a matching thin gold chain. She had an attractive face, Kate thought, with full lips and high cheek bones. Her smile was inviting.

"You must be Katherine Gifford. Welcome. I'm Dr. Zuckerman. Most people call me Dr. Leah." She stepped forward, her hand outstretched.

Kate rose and took it. It felt warm. Kate followed the doctor into the inner office and looked around. In one corner of the room were a desk, a chair and a couple of file cabinets. In the other corner were a sofa and two armchairs. The colors reflected those in the outer office; beige and cream with touches of orange and turquoise; attractive but understated.

"Please sit down." Dr. Zuckerman gestured to an armchair. Kate smiled, uncertain, looking to the right and left, and then sat down on the sofa. She was still shivering. She rubbed her arms.

"You look like you're freezing. I'm sorry about the air conditioning. Sometimes they have it set too high. Let me get you a sweater." The doctor opened a cupboard and rummaged around, then pulled out a sweatshirt with the words *Sunshine Girl* printed on the front over a winking yellow sun.

She laughed and handed it to Kate. "Sorry, this is all I've got."

Kate took it gratefully and slipped it on. "Thank you. Next time I'll remember to bring a sweater. I'm always cold." As she said it, she avoided the doctor's eyes.

Dr. Leah retrieved a pencil and a pad of paper from her desk and sat down across from Kate. Kate noticed a wedding ring and sapphire engagement ring on the doctor's left hand.

"I took a couple of notes when you called. You live on South Street, right here in Key West." She looked up, raising her eyebrows.

Kate nodded.

"May I ask how you found out about me?"

"I was walking past and saw the name stenciled on the outside door. That was a few weeks ago. It took me a while to get the nerve up to call for an appointment." She mumbled the last part, and Dr. Zuckerman leaned forward to catch her words.

The doctor gave her an encouraging smile. "I'm glad you did. Have you lived here long? Lots of us are transplants."

"No...yes, actually I've only been here for about five months. I moved down from Milwaukee." That was what Kate told anyone who asked. She'd eradicated Lakeland from her mind.

The doctor wrote something in her notebook and then looked up. "Tell me why you decided to come in for therapy."

Kate couldn't answer. She swallowed several times, twisting her thin fingers together. The silence was deafening. She felt like she might suffocate. The room began to spin and she lost consciousness.

Chapter 9   Cici
March, then

Cici Arnaud had changed her name. It hadn't been that difficult. She was using Oscar's last name now: Lebon. It meant "the good" in French. When she proposed the change to Oscar, he'd looked at her long and hard. Then he'd said, "Cécile, you know, you have always been like a daughter to me. Use my name if you would like. It's yours, *ma poulette*."

She could have chosen any name but using Oscar's made her feel as though she was still connected to her beginnings, to her roots. He had been part of her life since she was five, when her father died. She felt different with a new name. No one could find her now. She could reinvent herself.

For weeks after the accident, the Chicago papers had written articles about the tragedy. Back then her name was a household word in Lakeland.

"Cécile Arnaud is the one who killed the little girl on Ridge and Lakeland."

"Arnaud? What kind of name is that?"

"It's French. She was a teacher at the high school but after the accident she never came back. Probably feeling too guilty."

"She didn't fulfill her contract?"

"No, just left the school in the lurch."

"Pretty irresponsible, but still…"

"Well, I heard she'd been given the boot. They weren't hiring her back."

"There was probably something more to it. Maybe she had violent tendencies."

"Yeah, you never know. She might have been driving too fast and could have avoided the kid?"

She imagined these conversations and wallowed in anguish. Even though she had fled Lakeland High School, fled her friends and acquaintances, she couldn't escape the imaginings and she couldn't escape herself.

Last February after the accident Cici had asked a police officer to drive her to the Lakeland train station. She told him she couldn't drive, that she would never drive again. They had agreed to take her Jeep to a nearby lot. From the Metra train, she'd taken the "L" and then trudged the few blocks to La Pâtisserie Gourmande, her mother's bakery. Deep snow blanketed the streets, deadening all sounds. Chicago was an empty wasteland, as was her heart. In her memories, she saw herself; a solitary black figure walking in the white, white world, the courier of death.

When she finally arrived at the bakery, all was dark. She went around back to the alley. Under the street light she fumbled for her key. At last she managed to open the back door. In the vestibule she hung up her sopping coat and kicked off her ruined shoes. A wooden staircase led up to the apartment. Under the stairs was a door that led down to the ovens. Cici knew Oscar was down there, making croissants and baguettes for the early morning customers. She opened the door and crept down the stairs towards the light.

"Oscar." Her voice wavered.

He turned from sliding a loaf of bread into the brick oven and stepped back in surprise. "Cici, what's happened? Why are you here?" His warm dark eyes registered surprise and concern.

Something about the warmth and his kind face unhinged her. She collapsed into his floury, sweaty arms, crying helplessly. "I didn't mean to do it. It was an accident. I killed a little girl."

Chapter 10 Kate

January, now

Kate awoke. She was stretched out on the sofa in the doctor's office, her head on one pillow and her feet on another. A light blue blanket covered her body. She felt as though she had been deep asleep, not just out for a minute or two. Dr. Zuckerman was looking at her, brown eyes full of empathy and kindness.

"I'm sorry. I don't know what happened." Kate's voice was raspy and painfully apologetic.

"Don't worry. These things happen. Just rest for a few minutes."

Kate shut her eyes and felt the pain washing over her. She had been tamping it down, forcing it into her subconscious. But Dr. Leah's question had opened the floodgates. She didn't dare respond until she'd gained control of herself.

"Let me get you some water, or maybe tea. Would you like a hot cup of tea? I can make it."

"Okay, yes. That would be nice."

"I'll be back in a jiff. I've got to go down the hall to the kitchen."

Kate heard the door open and shut. Then there was silence. Could she go through with this? If one question had made her pass out, she wouldn't be able to withstand a barrage of them. This was a bad idea. She had to get out of here. Slowly she sat up, testing herself to see if she still felt dizzy. The room stayed steady. She stood up. So far, so good.

Quickly, she folded the blanket and placed it on the sofa. She pulled off the sweatshirt and folded it, then set it neatly on top of the blanket. She grabbed her purse, walked quickly to the door and pulled it open. In a flash, she was across the waiting room and out into the hallway. In the sun-filled corridor, she looked both ways. No one was around. She ran to the glass door that led out to the street. At last she was safe. The sun beat down on her; it was eighty-five degrees. Heat. Anonymity. Safety.

When Leah Zuckerman got back with the tea and a small packet of cookies from the vending machine, her patient was gone. She shouldn't have left her alone. She knew better. But the woman—Katherine?—was so painfully thin. Leah's first thought was that she'd passed out because of hunger. Maybe she hadn't had anything to eat that day. Leah sat down at her desk and took a sip of the tea. Earl Grey, her favorite. She often had tea in the afternoon, even in tropical Key West.

She thought about her new patient. This woman was in crisis. Her skin had looked unnaturally pale, especially for a Florida resident. Above sharp cheek bones, her startling green eyes were surrounded by dark circles. She was so painfully thin, emaciated really. Leah thought about the woman's hair. It had been dyed black; an unattractive hue that intensified her pale skin. Katherine Gifford was a combination of black and white; black hair, black clothes and white skin. No color in her anywhere.

She looked over at the sofa and the neatly folded blanket and sweatshirt. Then something caught her eye—a glimmer against the beige carpet. She got up and walked over to the sofa. Near it on the floor lay a heart-shaped silver locket on a silver chain.

She picked it up and used her fingernail to lift the cover. Inside the locket was a picture of a little girl with blond hair.

Chapter 11   Cici
March through May, then

Cici spent the first month after the accident mainly in bed, unable to read, watch TV, or think clearly. Time flew by without bringing her along. One minute it was nine in the morning and then it was noon. Her mother brought her homemade soups and crusty bread. Gently, she encouraged Cici to get up and take a shower. *"Ma chérie, il faut que tu te lèves. Prends une douche, lave-toi les cheveux."*

Cici's mother was a small, compact woman, with dark brown hair pulled into a neat bun. She wore simple dresses, almost always covered by a starched white apron with red and blue trim. Her dark eyes were bright and inquiring. Her mouth formed an easy smile. There were wrinkles around her eyes and lips. Cici knew her life had not always been easy. She had spent much of it working seven days a week.

In the early evening, Maman would enter her room; sit on the bed and smooth strands of hair off Cici's forehead. *"Tu n'étais pas responsable. Ce n'était pas de ta faute. Tu vas t'en remettre. Je t'assure."* It will be all right. It wasn't your fault. It was her mantra each evening.

The nights were the worst. In some nightmares Cici was back in her red Jeep plunging through snowdrift after snowdrift, each time feeling a soft bump in the road. Other times, she was walking in a world of swirling cotton. The spinning clouds of long white strands threatened to smother her, and she woke up beating the air with her hands.

One night, trembling and drenched with sweat, she slipped out of bed and pulled on a tee-shirt and sweatpants. Then she went down to the basement to help Oscar with the night time baking. He accepted her presence with a nod. They didn't talk much. Through gesture and example, he taught her how to mix the dough and proof it. Over the next few weeks she learned to roll a perfect croissant or a crispy *pain au chocolat* with a bar of chocolate nestled in its interior. They baked *baguettes, ficelles and pain de campagne*. Cici learned the secret to making light and delicious *macarons*, which were the rage in France and were taking over Chicago. Apple tarts and chocolate éclairs, and so much more.

When her mother came down with chicory-laced café au lait in the early morning, the three of them would sit down at the little table in the back, eat a freshly made croissant and sip the coffee and warm milk from large blue bowls. Their talk was quiet and easy. This was a good time of the day. Afterwards, Cici would mount the stairs to the second floor apartment, fall into bed and sleep for a few hours out of pure exhaustion.

After a month, Principal Myra Wilkins called. "Hello, Cécile. How are you feeling?"

Cici couldn't respond. She was sweating profusely. Her breath came in small gasps.

"Cécile, are you there?" There was a hint of irritation in Myra's voice.

Cici took a deep breath and cleared her throat. "I'm here, Dr. Wilkins."

"We're planning on you being back at school on Monday. Right? Your month of rest and relaxation is over. You need to get yourself back on track. It's too bad about the little girl, but there are a hundred and twenty students here at Lakeland that depend on you to finish out the school year."

Cici only heard the words 'little girl.' Her mind was spinning out of control and her mouth went dry. She couldn't respond.

As it turned out, Cici never did return to Lakeland. At first, the school district threatened to sue her for breach of contract, but eventually they let it go.

During the day, her mother's friend Héloïse came to work in the shop. She was a pastry chef and helped in the baking as well as manning the cash register. Cici lay in bed, listening to the goings-on from below: the bell at the door announcing the arrival of a customer, murmurs punctuated by Héloïse's booming laughter, Héloïse and Maman chatting as if they were having a party.

As the weeks progressed, Cici felt guilty just lying around. She had always helped out in the bakery on weekends and during the summer. One day she ventured downstairs in the late afternoon and told Maman to go upstairs and take a break. Spending time with Héloïse was comforting. With her it was as though the accident had never happened.

One afternoon late in the day, Cici was folding a pink square box. Mrs. Butterfield had decided on a chocolate mocha cake. Mrs. B. was a pink-faced, square-shaped lady who often stopped by on the way home from work for a box of pastries. She handed Héloïse her credit card as she chatted away, her voice loud and gushing.

"We've got my niece and her little girl coming for supper tonight."

"That ought to be fun," Héloïse extracted the receipt from the register and handed Mrs. Butterfield a pen. "Is this the niece who lives in Evanston?"

As she signed the receipt Mrs. B kept on talking. "Yes, Paula. Her husband is out of town so I said why don't you come down with Jilly for dinner. Jilly is just about three and she's a holy terror but I feel sorry for my niece. Paula is seven months pregnant and as big as a house. Jilly just runs her ragged." Mrs. B. shook her head. "Of course, at my house I don't let that little missy do whatever she wants. I have rules; not like the younger generation." She shot a glance at Cici and kept talking. "Why just last week, that little dickens ran across the street chasing a ball. Almost got herself killed."

At that, there was a terrible crash as the chocolate cake went sailing to the floor. Somehow it had slid sideways out of Cici's hands and landed upside down. The rich mocha cream had splattered everywhere behind the counter.

This stopped Mrs. B's incessant chatter. Her eyes popped and her mouth formed a perfect "O." "My goodness, what happened, girl? What a mess!" She leaned her bulk against the counter so she could take a look.

Cici turned pasty white and fled the room.

Héloïse smiled apologetically, "Let me box up another cake. There's another one right here in the display case."

Chapter 12   Kate
January, now

Kate nearly ran down the street. Before turning right at the next corner she looked back to make sure Dr. Leah wasn't in hot pursuit. After a couple of blocks she slowed down. Her fears were ridiculous. That woman was not going to follow her. She probably had another patient lined up. Kate would send her a check for the appointment even though they had barely spoken.

At the light she turned left and was soon in front of C & N Interiors. The display windows on each side of the door exhibited antique furniture. To the right was a Queen Anne dressing table with cabriole legs. Beside it stood a matching chair with a pink-and-cream striped satin seat. To the left was a set of Regency Bergère chairs in deep brown leather and a rosewood and gilt revolving bookstand. She knew these items well, since she had recently staged those display windows. As she opened the door, she heard the chime go off down the hall. She was safe.

Kate stood in the middle of the room and closed her eyes, getting her bearings, taking deep breaths.

"Hello, it's you. We thought we had a customer." A voice boomed.

She opened her eyes and saw Cyril.   He was frowning at her. "Hey, are you all right? I thought you weren't coming back this afternoon?"

"Thank goodness she did." Neil came down the hall, his cane clicking as he walked. "Tonight we're going to celebrate and you're coming with us."

They stared at her expectantly. "What are you celebrating?" she asked.

Cyril beamed. "The Morrisons' decision to let us do their entire house…four bedrooms, living room, dining room…"

"And even the pool area," Neal chimed in. He and Cyril often finished each other's sentences.

"Wow, that's fabulous," Kate said.

"And we owe it all to you, my dear," Cyril told her. "If you hadn't ensnared them when they came in looking for an antique lamp, this never would have happened."

"So we're going to Pastificio, the Italian restaurant down the street and you're coming with us." Neil sat down in a nearby chair and placed his cane across his knees.

"I'm so happy for both of you." She felt the stress of the afternoon dissipate. These two men had become her dear friends. They accepted her and asked few questions. Cyril and Neil had been living together for twenty years. Cyril was opinionated, flamboyant, temperamental, yet quick to laugh and easy to love. Neil was the calm one, gentle, kind and sweet. She could think of a million adjectives for each of them. "But I don't know if I'm up to dinner. Why don't you guys go without me?"

"No, no, no," Cyril said. "It's been decided. You go home and dress up in your finery. We'll meet you there at six sharp." He shooed her out the door.

It was four blocks to her walk-up, a studio in a Victorian house that had been broken up into four apartments. Hers was the smallest, tucked up under the eaves. She rarely ran into the other tenants. When she did, they smiled and addressed each other in platitudes: "Hi…How are you…Have a nice day," and so on.

The entrance to her place was in the back. She stopped by the front door to collect her mail and saw a handwritten sign posted in the entryway: "Notice to tenants. This building has been sold. It will be converted into a single-family home. All contracts are null and void. Residents have sixty days to vacate the premises. Please contact Liberty Realty for details."

Kate stared at the sign. It took a moment before the information sank in. Great, just great. Now she would have to find another place to live. The thought of moving her few meager possessions seemed monumental. She liked this studio. It was hidden away from the world and only a short walk over to the shop. She sighed, feeling exhausted.

Inside the small foyer were four mailboxes. Hers was usually empty but today a white envelope stuck out through the slot. She took it out. It was addressed to K. Gifford in slanted script. In the right-hand corner was printed the Carepath Grocery logo. Probably another hate letter from Sam. She didn't have a computer and he couldn't get to her except through the mail. Often she just threw the letters away. Why did he keep torturing her? He had gotten everything: the house, the furniture, the savings account. And Timmy. She hadn't contested the divorce decree. She knew she had been a bad mother. She hadn't watched her children. She had been drinking and on the Internet. She had let her little girl die. She reminded herself of this every single day.

Kate leaned against the grimy, paint-chipped wall and closed her eyes. She had already passed out once today. She stayed there with her eyes closed waiting for the dizziness to pass. Then she looked at the envelope and spotted handwritten initials in the top corner: *DPT.* Daniella Pojoli Tripp. Sam had married Daniella immediately after the divorce.

Kate went outside and around to the back. She climbed the two flights of stairs to her apartment, unlocked the door and went inside. The studio felt warm and stuffy. She opened the windows to create a breeze, then looked around. Her bed was against one wall, a sofa against the other. A folding card table and two straight-backed chairs stood in the middle of the room. The kitchen was merely a counter with a microwave, sink, small fridge and a set of cupboards. There was a postage-stamp bathroom with a tiny shower stall. It wasn't much, but this place had become home.

Kate opened a kitchen drawer and took out a knife. Carefully she slit open the envelope. Inside was a folded piece of paper. With trepidation she slipped the paper out and unfolded it.

The paper was a child's drawing, complete with yellow sun, blue sky, a house and a tree. On the ground was a big man, a big woman and a little boy. In the sky were two figures wearing wings, a lady with long red hair and a little girl with blond curls. There was no message attached.

Kate sat down on her bed staring at the picture. With her fingers she traced the lines. Dear little Timmy, this was as close as she could get. She clutched the picture to her breast, tears streaming down her face.

Chapter 13   Cici

August, then

By late August, Cécile was getting those back-to-school feelings that had been part of her life since kindergarten. Fall had always represented a new beginning. As a girl she had loved the fresh, clean notebooks, sharp pencils and new shiny backpack. As a teacher she had been eager to dive into the new school year and excited to prepare a challenging curriculum. The great thing about teaching was that each year gave her a chance to start anew.

This year she wasn't going anywhere. She was grateful to Maman and Oscar for being so patient with her. The last six months had been difficult for all of them.

She had no job and no prospects. She could live in her childhood bedroom forever, helping out in the bakery and maybe taking it over some day, but a restless part of her needed to get back out on her own. Her nightmares continued, along with terrible dark days when depression rolled over her like a heavy, wet blanket. As summer turned to autumn, she often dreamed of escape from Chicago and the looming winter. She didn't think she could bear the horror of a snowstorm.

One morning at dawn, Cici and Oscar ferried up the warm croissants and breads and arranged them behind the counter. Then they went upstairs to the apartment. Maman had prepared the coffee and they took it outside to the deck to sit in the cool morning air. The lone maple tree in the small backyard was bright with fall colors. Its branches reached over the deck. After the coffee, Maman went downstairs and Oscar and Cici sat companionably. As always after morning coffee, Oscar took out a Gitane and lit up. He inhaled deeply and blew out a stream of smoke. Then he removed a bit of tobacco from his lip with his thumb and forefinger and turned to look at her. "I have a proposition to make to you. Would you like to move away and try something new?"

Cici looked at him, unsure how to respond. Was she so transparent? Could Oscar and her mother tell how restless she'd become? She hadn't wanted to say anything that would upset them. "Well…" she said without finishing her sentence.

"Remember my friend André? He came up here for a visit some years ago when you were a girl?"

She nodded, gazing up at the canopy of yellow leaves overhead. She mainly remembered a large, boisterous man and an evening of laughter around the dining table.

Oscar drew on his cigarette. "André owns a bakery in Key West, Florida. He needs help. Since his wife died he has had several employees, mainly Hispanic, but nothing has worked out. The people just didn't have a love of the art of baking. And Cici, *ma chèrie*, baking, it is an art."

She looked over at him and smiled. He had repeated that often this past winter when they'd worked together through the night.

"I thought you might enjoy going down there. André is a good person with a kind heart."

"To work down there at the bakery?"

He nodded, then took another puff and blew smoke rings into the air. "I own a house there. Did you know that?"

"No. I remember you went down there a couple of times."

"It's what they call a conch house. A small clapboard cottage with a porch across the front. I've been renting it all these years. It's going to be vacant and I'm offering it to you." He looked at her expectantly.

Cici couldn't quite process this turn of events. "You're telling me I can move down to Florida? To Key West?"

He nodded.

43

"That I would have a job with your friend André?"

Oscar nodded again. He was beaming.

"That I could get away from here?" Then she realized what she was saying. She didn't want to hurt his feelings. "But what about you and Maman, don't you need me? Have you talked to her?"

"Cici, your maman and I think it is time for you to move on. We will miss you terribly but we don't *need* you." His face reflected the tenderness he felt for her. "We both love you and we share in your suffering, *ma petite*. But we think you need to begin your life again…"

She felt tears coming on as she bent over and hugged Oscar in an awkward embrace.

Chapter 14   Kate
January, now

Kate lay on her bed pressing Timmy's drawing to her chest, staring up at the slanted roof overhead. How was Timmy? She thought of the red-haired woman with angel wings. Did her son think she was dead? What had Sam and Daniella been telling him? When she said goodbye, he'd been angry. He had turned away and run upstairs. Now she wondered if she had done the right thing. But during those months after Betsy's death, Sam had worn her down.

"Look at you," he'd snapped. "You're a slob and a drunk. You killed your daughter. You aren't going to kill Tim too."

She hadn't been able to fight back because he was right. She was a worthless human being. She didn't deserve to have children. The only thing that got her through those months was her prescription for Zoloft. She'd stopped drinking, but was dependent on her depression medication. It kept her barely sane.

Sam hired a nanny who moved into Betsy's room and watched Timmy while he was at work. The woman was British, a believer in firm discipline and a regimented day. Sam had given her total control. She shooed Kate out of the kitchen and up the stairs. When Timmy was home from kindergarten, the nanny would keep him in the playroom. She made it clear that Kate was not to enter. From upstairs Kate could hear Timmy crying but she would not go to him. She'd believed Sam when he said Timmy was better off without her. So she lay in bed, staring at the ceiling, day after day.

Some nights he came home late, entered their bedroom stealthily, and fell on her in bed. He covered her mouth with his hand as he ravaged her; tearing at her nightgown, scratching her breast and plunging into her again and again. She lay there motionless.

Other nights when Sam was home for dinner, he came up to the bedroom to change out of his suit. Those nights he was snide and manipulative, verbally tearing her to shreds. "You stupid bitch. All you do is lie around. Why did I ever marry you? Daniella will be a far better mother to my son."

Later downstairs, she would hear Timmy's small voice and his father's sharp rebuke. When Timmy was in bed she was allowed to enter his room and kiss him goodnight while the nanny watched from the doorway.

"You come to the park with me, Mommy," Timmy would beg.

"Mommy's sick, sweetie. She has to stay home in bed."

"But I want *you*." He glanced at the nanny. "I don't want *her*. She's not my mommy."

One day Sam brought divorce papers home for her to sign and she did so. She didn't fight him. She had killed her daughter. She couldn't be trusted with her son. Timmy would be better off with Daniella; someone competent and dependable, not a dithering idiot. She left a couple of months later, when Sam ordered her out.

Remembering those months didn't do any good. She'd better get up and take a shower if she was going to meet Cyril and Neil. She felt sweaty and sticky after her visit with the psychologist. Fear and tension had made her perspire profusely.   She got up, went to the bathroom and turned on the shower. Standing in front of the mirror, she pulled off her tank top.

There was nothing around her neck. The locket and its silver chain were gone. She picked up the tank top and shook it, but no locket fell out.

She went back to the main room and searched the floor and the day bed. No locket. Where had she lost it? When had she last seen it? She began to shake. The locket was all she had of Betsy. She had to find it. Remembering the afternoon, she knew she'd had it at Dr. Leah's office. It had to be somewhere between there and the apartment. She pulled her shirt back on and headed for the stairs.

Kate went down the staircase slowly, studying each worn wooden step as she went. Nothing. She went back around front and into the foyer with the mailboxes. Nothing. She retraced her steps to the shop. Cyril and Neil were no longer there. She used her key to open the front door and entered the dark interior. Carefully studying the floor, she made her way to the counter and back. Nothing. Her heart was beating a mile a minute. She had to find that necklace.

Outside she locked the shop and stood still, thinking. Cars passed and people walked by. *Come on, Kate. Get a hold of yourself. You'll find the locket. Think, think.* Where could it have fallen? Then it hit her. It must have fallen off when she was rushing down the street after racing out of the doctor's office.

She turned and took off down the sidewalk. Looking to the right and left as she went, down to the corner, then over. The sun was low in the sky now and the buildings and trees cast long shadows. The approaching darkness made her feel frantic. She had to find the necklace before dark. What if someone had picked it up?

When Kate arrived at the doctor's building, the glass door was locked. She banged on the door, yelling. "Is anyone there? Open up, I need to get in." Tears of frustration streamed down her cheeks. She kept banging and then sagged

47

against the door, her palm on the glass and her cheek smudging the surface. "Please open up." She sobbed.

A middle-aged couple walked by. They both looked concerned. "Can we help you?" The woman asked.

Kate straightened up and wiped her eyes with her palms. "I'm all right. Thanks."

They kept looking at her, uncertain. The man said, "Are you sure?"

"Yes, I'm fine." Kate headed back towards the antique shop, moving quickly, looking back periodically until the couple was no longer in view. She passed the shop and kept going toward her apartment, where she retrieved a flashlight and her phone. This time she had the presence of mind to lock her door when she headed back out.

Two more times she retraced her steps, hoping against hope that a bit of silver would flash on the sidewalk. Arriving at the office building a third time, she pulled out her phone and dialed the number for Dr. Leah Zuckerman that was printed in gold letters on the side panel of the door. The answering service picked up, and a woman's voice asked if she wanted to leave a message.

"No, I have to talk to Dr. Zuckerman, now. Please, I must talk to her."

"Is this an emergency, Miss?"

Kate's voice rose. "Yes, an emergency. Please, please. I must talk to her."

She heard murmurs as the woman talked to someone else. Then she came back on the line. "We don't like to bother the doctor in the evening, miss."

"Don't you fucking get it?" Kate shouted. "I have to talk to her now! It's a matter of life or death."

There was silence on the line. Then, sounding prim and unfriendly, the woman said, "Please give me your name and number and we will contact the doctor."

"It's Katherine Gifford." Too keyed up to thank her, she gave the woman her phone number. "Please tell her to call me right away."

The woman hung up without responding.

Kate sat down on the stoop outside the office building and waited for the call.

Chapter 15   Cici
September, then

Cici accepted Oscar's proposal. She spent several hours on the phone discussing the job with André. She would work in the Pâtisserie-Boulangerie from 7AM until 4PM. She would be in charge of the shop while André slept. She would make pastries: éclairs, religieuses, tartes, and so on. A daytime assistant would be working with her. His name was Napoléon and he was Haitian. André felt Napoléon had a lot of talent, but he didn't want to leave him in charge all day.

Once she'd made the decision to move, time passed quickly. Cici sold all of the furniture that Oscar had retrieved from her old apartment and stored in the garage. She only kept a few boxes of household necessities to send down to Key West. When she arrived there she would have to go out and buy a bed, a sofa and table and chairs. Oscar told her the house was unfurnished except for some outdoor furniture on the front porch and behind the house on the veranda.

As moving day approached Cici began to have misgivings. She'd felt safe and protected these last six months. Her life had taken on a comforting simplicity. Now everything would be new and she would be alone to face the demons kept at bay in the recesses of her psyche. But when she thought about the encroaching winter, she felt ready to go.

The morning of her departure was hard. Maman was being strong, her naturally easy-going manner replaced by a brusque, no-nonsense persona that Cici rarely saw. She banged the bowls of café au lait on the table and shoved the basket of croissants towards Oscar. "Hurry up. Help yourself. Where's the sugar? Someone has hidden the sugar."

"Maman, it's right here behind the milk jug."

Her mother only humphed in response and didn't look in her direction.

After an uncomfortable breakfast where no one dared say a thing, her mother got up and stomped into the kitchen. Cici cleared the table and went to put the dishes in the dishwasher. She found her mother scrubbing a pot from last night's Bon Voyage dinner, tears running down her cheeks. Cici put down the dishes, grasped her mother's shoulders and turned her around. They stood together hugging and crying.

"I'll be back. And you'll be coming down to visit. This isn't forever."

"*Je sais*. But I will miss you so much, *ma chèrie*. I do so worry about you."

"Don't worry. I've been through the worst of it. It'll work out."

The leave-taking had been painful and Cici almost changed her mind on the way to the airport. Was she doing the right thing? Was she running away instead of facing the murder she'd committed?

The flight to Miami was uneventful. When she arrived she looked for the large, boisterous man with blond hair and blue eyes that she vaguely remembered. As she scanned the crowd milling around the baggage area, a wiry black man came up to her; his face alight with a brilliant smile.

"You are Cécile Lebon, *oui*?" He spoke with a musical accent. This must be Napoléon.

"Yes, I am." She couldn't help but smile back.

"I am here to collect you. Monsieur André is out in the van. You come, please?"

He bent down and began picking up her luggage. He managed four bags and she took two others. They headed for the door. Outside, André Guerin stood beside a white van with

Guerin Pâtisserie-Boulangerie printed on the side in red and blue letters. There was a little beret on the "B."

"Mademoiselle Cécile, I am very glad to welcome you to Florida," André said with a deep sense of formality. He bent and kissed her hand.

"Thank you." She blushed and smiled at André and Napoléon. She felt as though she was stepping into a whole new world. The sun beat down on her head and a warm breeze caressed her bare arms.

The trip to Key West took nearly four and a half hours. Along the way André and Napoléon kept up a steady conversation. They pointed out sights, restaurants and superior fishing grounds. She listened, nodded and smiled. They didn't ply her with questions, but included her in their discussions. Most of their conversation was in English with a good sprinkling of French and Haitian patois.

At times she saw water on each side of the road. They went over a series of bridges and through small towns. She felt oddly relieved as the miles went by. She was leaving the mainland, leaving her past, leaving her sorrow behind.

They stopped along the way and had lunch in Islamorada at the Fish Company restaurant. Cici noted alligator, conch and dolphin on the menu. Things she had never tried before or even imagined eating. They had fried grouper sandwiches and iced tea. The fish was unbelievably delicious and the surroundings made her think of a movie set.

André and Napoléon told her about things to do in Key West: the Truman and Hemingway museums, the Butterfly Conservatory, and the Cabaret at La Te Da. That name got her laughing. "So tell me, do you attend performances and visit museums?"

They looked at each other and grinned. "Actually we don't," André admitted. "My life is work, work, work. But that is the life I chose."

"The Mondays, the patisserie, it is closed. Sometimes I take a promenade and visit a musée," Napoléon said, somewhat virtuously.

"I think you do a lot of sleeping on Mondays," André said, shaking his finger at Napoléon. "And a lot of fishing!" They both laughed.

"Well, I'm here to work as well," Cici said. "But on Mondays maybe I'll do some touristy stuff."

When the men started discussing the ins and outs of various fishing lures, Cici fell asleep lulled by their voices, a full stomach and the warm breeze.

She woke up just as they pulled in front of a yellow house with white trim. She rubbed her eyes and turned to look at André, who was smiling at her. "Voilà, we've arrived."

She turned back to look at the house. A white picket fence surrounded it. There was a porch across the front with two rocking chairs. On each side of the house were palm trees and some bushes that boasted a lush display of blue flowers. The house looked cozy. She fell in love with it instantly.

Napoleon went to the back and began taking out the suitcases. He and André each picked up three and gestured for Cici to open the gate. She pushed up on the metal handle and the gate swung open. They went across the miniature yard and up the steps. There was lattice work at each end of the porch and it was shady and cool. The white rocking chairs had blue and green plaid cushions.

André pulled out a key, opened the door and stood back. "Après vous, Mademoiselle."

She stepped into a small foyer. To her right was a staircase; to the left was a closet. Moving forward, she stepped into a large, rectangular room. At the far end, floor-to-ceiling windows looked out on a shady veranda. To the right was a kitchen with white cabinets and dark grey granite countertops.

An island with two stools separated the kitchen from the living area.

Nearer to the veranda against the wall sat a white linen sofa and two matching armchairs with bright pink-and-green striped pillows. Between them, a bamboo glass-topped table sported a fat porcelain lamp with a matching pink and green lampshade. The light oak floors shone, and a colorful rag rug lay under a round oak table with four chairs. In the center of the table stood a white pitcher filled with flowers. Cici turned and laughed at the two men who were watching her reactions. "It's so pretty, so cute...so cozy."

"Oscar, he wanted everything nice for you," André said.

"I'm just so surprised. I didn't know what to expect."

Her boxes from Chicago were stacked in a corner. Through a wide opening she saw an alcove with built-in bookshelves, a desk and cupboards. A window in the alcove looked out at more blue-flowered bushes. What were those flowers? They made her feel happy inside.

She went to the French windows and stepped out onto the veranda. A high fence covered by a cascade of pink bougainvillea surrounded the small backyard. Cici heard the gurgle of water in the small swimming pool surrounded by a wooden deck that held two chaise lounges with blue-and-white striped cushions. She felt as though she had gone to heaven right here on earth.

She looked back at Napoléon and André, who were trailing behind her, both beaming with expectation. They had obviously been in on the set-up and wanted to see her reaction to everything. She swung around, her arms in the air. "Everything is beautiful. Thank you both." She had tears in her eyes.

André looked uncomfortable. "We're going to take our leave now." He held out a set of keys and a tourist's map of

Key West. "This is your house here with the black X. See, this is the bakery marked with the other X. You just go down two blocks and then to the right four blocks. It's not far."

"That'll be an easy walk. Shall I be there tomorrow at six?"

"*Mais non*, take tomorrow to install yourself in the house. I will see you bright and early on Wednesday. Okay?"

"That would be great. I'll unpack, get my bearings and be ready to go on Wednesday. Thank you again for coming to get me, for lunch and for all that you've done." She accompanied them to the door.

André shook her hand and Napoléon tipped his hat. "*A bientôt*." And they were gone.

She stood still in the small foyer and closed her eyes, getting a feeling of the place. Already it felt like home. She listened to the sounds a house makes: the whir of the refrigerator, the creak of the floors, the breeze rustling the curtains. All new now, but soon they would become familiar.

She opened her eyes and started upstairs. The house had two bedrooms, each with an attached bath. The bedroom on the right was empty. To the left was the room Oscar had outfitted for her. An antique honeycomb quilt covered the queen-size bed. On each bedside table were graceful lamps made from Chinese vases. White curtains fluttered at the windows. She moved into the bathroom, which was painted yellow and white. There were yellow and turquoise striped towels on the rack and a shower curtain covered with daisies. Oscar had thought of everything. He had put his heart and soul into this little house. How could she ever repay him?

Down a short hallway, she found another door. It led into an unfinished room that served as an attic of sorts. It had windows and could have been made into a third bedroom. For the moment, it would do to hold her empty luggage and boxes once she'd unpacked.

Back downstairs, she looked in the refrigerator and found a bag of oranges. On the counter was a juicer. In a jiff she had squeezed a big glass of orange juice, and she was ready to attack her suitcases.

Chapter 16   Leah

January, Now

Leah Zuckerman looked across the table at Robert. He was glued to the screen of his cell phone. She smiled to herself. So much for a romantic dinner for two. They were down at the harbor at the Commodore. They had both ordered the snapper.

From their table Leah could see the boats settled in their berths for the night. Water lapped against the wooden moorings and seagulls cut through the sky. They were the town criers announcing the end of the day and heralding the evening's arrival. A light breeze wafted over her, gentle fingers of night. Leah loved the beauty and mystery of dusk. She let her mind settle on the present moment.

Somewhere she'd read that this was the secret to happiness: to live with gratitude for the past, mindfulness of the present and optimism for the future. As she remembered it, *mindfulness* was living fully in the present and appreciating it. This could be achieved through meditation or yoga or simply concentrating on the moment. Well, if that were true, she was enjoying this moment and she *was* happy.

The waiter arrived with their sautéed yellowtail snapper. Once the plate was set before him, Robert put down his phone, shook out his napkin and placed it on his lap.

"Sorry." His smile was apologetic. "Too much going on right now...one of my showings for tomorrow wants to see the house tonight."

"How much time have you got?"

"A good hour." He reached over and turned off his phone. "Now, I'm all yours."

Robert owned a midsize real estate company that dealt with houses primarily in Key West, though he had listings throughout the Keys. Because of the distances, he had offices in Marathon, Islamorada and Key Largo. Three women manned these smaller offices and there was always a looming crisis that needed his attention.

Robert had an easy manner and was rarely ruffled by the vagaries of life. "Easy come, easy go...take life as it comes...plain sailing...it's a piece of cake." Those were his mantras. Leah had never seen him really angry. Not to say that he wasn't a shark where his business was concerned, but he rarely let things get to him.

He was a little taller than she, with bright blue eyes that crinkled at the corners. At thirty-six his hair was getting a little thin on top but it didn't seem to bother him. He had smooth fine-grained skin that most women would die for. With an athletic build and an energetic personality, he exuded a zest for life. Leah was still very much in love with him.

Born in Akron, Ohio, she'd come down to Key West on a research grant. The second night there she met Robert Smith and that was that. Love at first sight just like in the movies. After three months of dating they moved in together. Two years later they were married, though Leah kept her maiden name professionally. They moved at the same rhythm, as if life was a dance and they were spinning through it together.

Robert had joined his father's real estate business and he loved it. His father proudly added him to the company's signage: Smith and Smith Realty. Initially, they'd had differences of opinion about how things should be done, but these issues had been ironed out and they had worked side by side for several years. Last May Robert Senior had died suddenly of a heart attack. Now Leah's Robert found himself sole proprietor of the company.

"What happened with you today?" He picked up his fork and knife.

"I had an unsettling experience. A young woman, a new patient, came in for an appointment." Leah looked out at the water lapping the wooden pilings. "Robert, she looked like a ghost. White, white skin, black clothes and dyed black hair…just a wraith."

"Wraith?" He liked ribbing her about her vocabulary.

Leah smiled. "Yes, a ghost, and so thin. Anyway, I'd just started the session, asking her why she wanted therapy, and she fainted. Just like that."

"Do you think she's on drugs?"

"No, nothing like that. I think she couldn't handle the question emotionally. When she came around, I suggested a cup of tea. She told me she was cold when she came in and I thought I could get her some tea and cookies. You know, warm her up and feed her something. So I went down to the kitchenette and left her alone. That was my big mistake. When I came back she was gone." She fingered the stem of her wine glass.

"You've got her name, right? You could track her down?"

"Yes, I suppose I could. She was a bundle of nerves and probably needs to talk to somebody…which is why she came to me."

"Well, you can't force anyone into therapy. You of all people know that. If she's not too embarrassed she'll probably be back."

"You're right, I just feel like I flubbed up."

"You mean, you bollixed it?" He reached out and took her hand.

"Yes. I screwed up." Her smile wavered. Leah always cared too much about her patients. She picked up her fork and cut a small bite of fish. "What about you, anything new?"

"You know that rental on Olivia Street, the yellow one with the porch?"

"Yes, I always liked that little cottage."

"Well, last fall the owner's daughter or niece moved in so it went off the market. This girl works at the French bakery, the Guérin pastry shop."

"You mean, the Guérin Pâtisserie-Boulangerie." Leah's pronunciation was perfect. She had had years of French in high school and college as well as a junior year abroad in Aix-en-Provence. "I go in there sometimes for baguettes and that strawberry tart you love."

Robert nodded. "Anyway, the daughter or niece wants a roommate. Probably needs help with the payments."

"Or maybe she's just lonely. How many bedrooms are there?"

"Two, each with a full bath. She called today and talked to Sherry. We're going to put an ad in the Keynoter next week."

They continued eating and talking as the sun set and the moon came up over the water. Over coffee Robert turned on his phone and then looked up at Leah. "How does next week look to you? How about we take a few days off and drive to Islamorada for a mini-vacation." He consulted his phone. "I could get away on Monday and Tuesday."

Normally, Leah didn't see patients on Monday. That was her and Robert's day together. "I'll check my appointment book. Maybe I could move Tuesday's appointments around."

As they were getting ready to leave, Leah's phone rang. Robert bent over and kissed her lips and then waved a silent goodbye. He had to get to his showing.

"Dr. Zuckerman?" It was the answering service.

"Yes, speaking."

"Sorry to bother you, but you have a patient who said she needs to talk to you. She's pretty frantic."

60

"What's her name?"

"Katherine Gifford. I told her I would give you her number. She sounds really upset."

"Okay, thanks. What's the number?"

Ten minutes later, Leah pulled up in front of the office building. The street was dark except for a light illuminating the foyer and front steps. Under the light a woman sat, legs pulled up against her chest and head resting on her knees. She seemed small and childlike. Leah got out of the car and approached her cautiously. "Hello, Katherine." She kept her voice low and sympathetic. Not knowing how the woman would respond she moved closer and sat down on the steps a few feet away. Sometimes patients reacted violently when approached too quickly.

Katherine looked up at her slowly, taking a moment to focus. She looked exhausted; dark circles ringed her eyes "Have you got it with you?"

"Yes." Leah opened her purse and pulled out the envelope with the necklace. She handed it to Katherine.

Like a starving animal, Katherine ripped open the envelope and pulled out the silver chain and locket. She clutched it to her chest, breathing in rapid gulps. Then she used her thumbnail to open the locket. For a long moment she stared at the picture inside as though devouring it. Then she closed the silver heart and rubbed it against her cheek. After a moment she drew the chain over her head and tucked the locket inside her shirt. She turned to Leah and said, "Thank you." Slow, tired tears made their way down her cheeks.

"You're welcome."

"She's my daughter." Katherine stared out at the empty, dark street. "It's all I have."

"Yes."

"She's gone." The slow tears dripped from her chin to her hands that were clutched in her lap.

Leah kept still.

"He got rid of everything else…all her clothes, her toys, her favorite doll."

Leah focused on the shifting shadows across the street that moved with the breeze.

"One night he hit me and ripped the chain off my neck and threw the locket away but I found it."

"Yes."

Katherine turned and looked into Leah's eyes. "He knew I killed her." She covered her face with her hands and started sobbing quietly.

Leah stayed still for a moment. Then she moved closer and touched Katherine's arm. The woman didn't flinch. "Have you talked with someone about this?"

Katherine shuddered and took several ragged breaths. "No. I'm too ashamed."

"I think you need to come back and see me. I think you need to talk. Will you do that?"

"Uh-huh."

They sat together for a few more minutes as Katherine's tears subsided.

Leah looked up and down the block. "Have you got a car here?"

"No, I walk everywhere or take the bus."

"Let me drive you home, okay?"

"I could walk. It's not far."

"Come on, I'd like to get you home safe." Leah took Katherine's elbow and helped her stand up. They walked together to the car.

Five minutes later Leah pulled up in front of the house where Katherine lived. She got out and accompanied Katherine through the back garden and watched her ascend the stairs. "Good night, Katherine. Remember to call me tomorrow. I can help you."

"Yes, I promise," Katherine said wearily.

Back in the car Leah watched a few minutes until the lights went on in the room up under the roof. Then she drove home slowly, feeling the weight of the world on her shoulders.

Chapter 17   Cici
September, then

Cici woke up to birds twittering and warm sunshine dancing through the white lace curtains. She stretched and smiled to herself. Could she really be in Florida starting a brand new life? It was too good to be true. She got out of bed and took a peek out the open window. She heard the good-morning sounds of a city rousing itself...traffic, voices, smells. Chicago had special morning sounds too but they were different.

She pulled on some shorts and a tee-shirt and went down to make coffee. On the counter was a straw basket with fresh croissants, rolls and a small pot of raspberry jam. There was a note: *Sorry to have invaded your home without permission but I worried myself about your breakfast. Bonne Journée   André   À demain.*

She carried her coffee and basket out to the patio and sat down at the little table. Out here, she could smell the sea air and listen to the gurgle of the fountain that fed the small pool. After devouring both a croissant and a roll and downing two cups of coffee, Cici picked up the phone and called home.

"*Salut*, Maman. I'm here having breakfast and I'm thinking about you and Oscar. I miss you both."

"*Bonjour, ma chèrie*, we were just talking about you. It's warm today and we're sitting out on the deck."

"Well, I'm sitting outside too. It's heavenly."

"What are you going to do today?"

"I'm not starting at the bakery until tomorrow so today I'm unpacking. Then I thought I'd go for a walk and get a sense of the town. André gave me a map."

"That sounds like a good plan. But don't tire yourself out."

"Maman, when was the last time you took a day off? You should follow your own advice. "

"That's different." Cici could hear the smile in her voice. "Here, I'm going to pass the phone to Oscar. *Je t'embrasse.*"

Oscar's voice was jovial. "*Bonjour, ma petite.* How was the trip down?"

"Oh, Oscar. Everything went very well. I like André and Napoléon and they are both so nice. Today, someone brought me a surprise breakfast basket." She heard him chuckle. "But Oscar, I don't know how to thank you enough for everything you did with the house. I just love it. It's perfect."

"Did you like the white sofa? I thought that was a good color. You can change things with different-colored pillows. Your maman and André, we all planned it together."

She could hear him saying something to her mother across the miles. Suddenly a wave of loneliness swept over her. She could feel her eyes smarting, and her voice trembled. "The white sofa is perfect. Thank you." She took a breath. "I better hang up now and get to work. *Je vous embrasse tous les deux.*" She hung up quickly. The last thing she wanted to do was burst into tears.

Cici spent the morning unpacking and arranging pots and pans, dishes and silverware in the kitchen. In one box she found six carefully folded aprons similar to the ones her mother wore in the bakery. They were crisp white cotton with blue and red trim. Her mother must have slipped them in. This brought on another wave of nostalgia. She would have to write a special note to thank Maman.

Next she filled the bookshelves in the library alcove carefully lining up her notebooks. Upstairs, she began to unpack her clothes when it hit her that she would never wear most of them down here in Key West. Why had she even packed the sweaters, corduroy pants, heavy shoes and boots? She put them back in the boxes and shoved them into the empty attic room.

What remained of her wardrobe was pretty paltry. She had some comfortable old shorts and tee-shirts as well as several dresses too fancy for everyday wear. She needed a Florida wardrobe. For the first time in eight months, she felt like going out on a shopping spree. After a quick shower she was out the door with map in hand.

Chapter 18   Kate
January, now

Kate arrived at the shop early the next morning. Cyril and Neil walked in while she was dusting and cleaning. She had gone outside with a squeegee and washed the windows. Now she was cleaning the display case in the front room. She felt guilty about letting them down, never showing up for their celebration dinner, and in response she was buzzing around the shop like a dervish.

"I'm so, so sorry about last night," she said when they came in.

"We were worried about you," Neil said quietly.

"I didn't mean to blow you off. Something terrible happened. I lost my locket. And I was frantic. I came back here and then I retraced my steps to Dr. Zuckerman's office. I was kind of crazy." They were looking at her, clearly not quite understanding, as she rattled on. "So I finally called the doctor and she had it and she brought it to me and then she drove me home. And..." Kate paused, briefly overcome with emotion. "I should have called you but it was late and I fell in bed with my clothes on." She held up the locket that gleamed against her black tee-shirt. "Here it is."

"I'm glad you found it, kiddo," Cyril said. "Next time, call us and we'll help you look. That's what friends are for, right?"

"Of course..." Her voice trailed off. "I was just so frantic." She twisted the dust rag in her fingers. "It's all I have...the locket, I mean."

They all stood there in silence. Cyril and Neil didn't know her story. She had kept everything secret since she'd started working there. They probably figured she'd fled a romance gone sour. But they seemed to like and trust her.

"I know that necklace is important to you, since you wear it every day." Neil looked at her, an unspoken question in the air. Katherine looked away and reached down to pick up a crystal vase. She gave it a vigorous rub.

"We'll be in the office doing some brainstorming. Then we've got an appointment with the Morrisons at eleven. You're welcome to come along if you'd like. It would be good to get your vibes on the house," Cyril said.

"What about the shop?"

"We can close it down for an hour. You're our number one consultant." Cyril wiggled his eyebrows at her and then turned to follow Neil down the hall.

Kate set the vase down, folded her dust rag and took a seat on the stool behind the counter. She gazed out at the quiet sun-dappled street, remembering her move down to Key West last July. She'd gotten the idea from the pictures Chet had sent her when they chatted online. The town seemed exotic: the water, the sunsets, the palm trees, the art colony. The perfect escape from the snow-clogged Midwest. And Key West was the last stop before stepping off into the ocean and leaving the US behind. She wanted to get as far from Lakeland as she could.

Although Chet's photos were the impetus for moving down to Florida, she'd made no effort to contact him. She hadn't logged on to a computer since last February. In her tangled mind she connected Chet with Betsy's death. As though he had colluded with her, as though he were as guilty as she in her daughter's demise. And yet she had chosen Key West.

After finding the studio apartment, she'd hunted for a job. She wasn't qualified to do much since she hadn't finished college. There was a lot of competition in the job market and salaries were low. After many disappointments, she got hired to clean rooms in a small hotel. Cleaning toilets and changing soiled sheets seemed appropriate work for a daughter-killer. The owner was a slave driver who consistently found fault in her work. The other women working there were Hispanic and didn't speak much English. It was a lonely time but she felt she deserved to be alone and unhappy.

Kate worked the early shift. After changing out of her uniform and donning her black garb, she walked slowly home. Sometimes she stopped at the library on Flemming to get a book or at the local mini mart. She subsisted on oatmeal, fruit, raw vegetables and cheese quesadillas…anything she could cook in the microwave; she had stopped caring about food.

In her meanderings, she often walked by C & N Interiors. Sometimes she stopped and gazed in the windows. She felt drawn to them, even though she knew little about decorating and antiques. Sometimes there were rolls of wallpaper lined up like soldiers across the back wall. Other times a length of silky fabric was draped over a chair. She found the colors and designs arresting.

One day she saw a sign propped in the window: *Salesgirl Wanted.* Without thinking, she entered the shop. The showroom was musty and dust particles floated in the oblique rays of sunlight. Furniture, mirrors and all manner of *objets d'art* were scattered haphazardly throughout the room. Neil—though she hadn't known his name then—was seated on this very same stool polishing a silver spoon.

"I wondered if we'd see you today." He stopped rubbing and looked up at her, his eyes dancing.

Kate stood there speechless.

"You might be the girl we're looking for. You're the only person consistently entranced by our shop windows."

"Oh?" She managed to say.

"I've seen you, standing there in the afternoons, gazing at them."

"You have?"

"So, are you interested in the sales job? It's yours if you want it."

And so Kate had miraculously found this job with these two kindly gentlemen.

Chapter 19   Cici
September, then

Cici took a moment to study the map and turned left on to Olivia Street. There was a small grocery store at the corner with a nice selection of fruits and vegetables. Wandering along quiet streets, she found a coffee shop, a drycleaners and a used-books store. Several blocks further she found herself on Duval Street. The street was bustling with tourists. There were the usual shops with tee-shirts, sunglasses and ice cream. She peered into the Margaritaville bar. Even at this hour there was a lot of action. She decided she would come back some evening.

At the end of the street, she went into another shop that carried bathing suits and cover-ups. She was attracted by a green-sprigged dress in the window. A young woman with spiked hair came around from behind the counter. She wore a scooped-neck, sleeveless sheath. It was navy blue with white trim and hit her just above the knee. Cici thought it was exactly the dress she would like to have along with the green one.

The girl had an easy, open smile. "What can I help you with?"

"I just moved down here yesterday. I need to buy some Florida clothes: shorts, shirts, skirts, dresses at a reasonable price." Cici felt scruffy in her tired jean shorts and wrinkled tee-shirt. Strands of hair were poking out of her ponytail and her nails were rough and broken from pulling open boxes.

The salesgirl had perfect make-up, perfect hair, and nails displaying sky-blue polish with little white flower appliqués. "What brought you down here? Are you an artist?"

Cici considered the question. "I suppose you could say so if you tasted one of my chocolate éclairs. Actually, I'm a baker. I'm going to be working at Guérin's, the French bakery."

"Oh, I love that place. My boyfriend and I go there on Sunday mornings." The girl looked Cici up and down. "I could help you out. I buy wholesale for some shops around here. I've got some merchandise in the back that I haven't moved yet. Want to take a look?"

"That would be great. So far I've only found stuff for tourists and for more than I want to spend."

"Come on. My name is Clarissa, by the way." She gestured toward a curtain in the back. Cici followed her through to a large storage room filled with racks and racks of clothes and boxes of sandals and shoes. "Why don't you look around?" Clarissa said. "Try things on. There's a mirror over there if you want to check yourself out."

"This is amazing. I like those white shorts." Cici pointed across the room to an open box.

"Listen. Since you're joining the workforce down here, I'll give you a deal. You can pay wholesale for whatever you find today. Okay?" Clarissa bent over and picked up a pair of yellow sandals. "Aren't these cute?"

"Oh gosh, that's super, and yeah they are cute."

"You look about a size two. The petite sizes are mainly along this wall."

Just then Cici heard a loud squawk. It sounded like a parrot or some other tropical bird. She looked around the storage room. Clarissa started to laugh. "That's my buzzer. Pretty annoying, isn't it? I'll leave you to it." She went back to the front of the store.

Cici spent over an hour trying on shorts, shirts, dresses and sandals. Periodically Clarissa came back and gave her opinion. "That looks really cute on you... Not that color, try on

72

the blue one…Way too big…Try these on, they're scrumptious."

At the end Cici had a pile of clothes, flip flops and sandals that were different from anything she'd ever bought. Up front, Clarissa did a quick inventory, scribbled some numbers on a pad and handed Cici the total.

"Are you sure this is right? I don't want to cheat you. It doesn't seem like near enough!" Cici said.

Clarissa grinned at her. "I told you it was wholesale. I feel good about this."

"If you're sure…" Cici handed Clarissa her credit card and then they packed up the clothes in three big shopping bags.

"Where's your car? You could bring it around back."

"I don't have a car." Cici hadn't even thought about getting the stuff home.

"How far away do you live?"

Cici told her where it was on Olivia Street. "I walked here and I've got to find my way home."

Clarissa scrunched up her face. "I know what we'll do. I'll drop the bags off on my way home. Will that work?"

"Do you mind? Won't it be out of your way?"

"No, actually it's on my way. Gloria is coming in at five for the evening shift so I'll be by your place at five-fifteen."

"I can't thank you enough. You've been so nice." Cici paused, looking sheepish. "Can I ask you where you got your hair cut?" She gestured to her long pony tail. "I think I might cut everything off."

"I go to the Smooth Sailing Salon. Here, let me show you on your map."

By five o'clock Cici was home and felt like a new person. When she opened the door to Clarissa's knock fifteen minutes later, Clarissa started to laugh. "Oh my god, what a change. You look great."

Cici did a pirouette. "I feel like Peter Pan. Or his sister." Her long dark hair was gone. In its place she had a pixie cut with a blond streak across her bangs.

"You know what? You look adorable." Clarissa turned her around. "You have small features and a perfect nose." She considered again. "It's actually kind of sexy."

Cici invited her in but Clarissa was meeting someone for dinner. "Let's get together another night!" She handed Cici the bags and gave her a wave.

Cici went upstairs and hung up her new skirts and dresses. She folded up the shorts and shirts and put them in the dresser. Then she went into the bathroom and looked at herself in the mirror, turning her head to the right and left. She barely recognized herself. With her diminutive stature, she could be taken for a boy.

Downstairs she took out a wine glass and opened a bottle of French Chablis that André had left for her. She took the glass out to the patio and lay down on the chaise. Overhead the fronds of the palm tree rustled in the breeze. Long rays of sun angled across the fence. The wine was crisp and cold.

This had been a crazy, wonderful day. She had spoiled herself. All of this change was exhilarating. She closed her eyes and breathed in deeply.

Then, abruptly, the dark, familiar feelings wrapped themselves around her heart like barbed wire, squeezing. Her breath came in gasps. The guilt always struck hardest in the early evening—the time of day it had all happened. She didn't have a right to be happy. She had killed a little girl, a little girl who would never know a sunny day in Key West.

Chapter 20   Kate
January, now

Kate had done some dusting and had repositioned the two Louis XV bergères. She sat down behind the counter where she had her own little antique desk. Here things were quiet. From the back she could hear Cyril and Neil bickering. They argued about every piece of furniture and every roll of wallpaper for every house they decorated, though never in front of a client. By the time they made their presentation, they'd already discussed, quarreled, shouted and eventually come to an agreement. At first Kate had worried when she heard them going at it, but they always ended up coming to a consensus and laughing together. Clearly, the arguments were was part of their creative process.

The bell over the door tinkled, and a woman with bouncing gold ringlets came into the shop. She wore a long flowered dress. Jangling silver bracelets wreathed both arms. Her perfume laid siege to the room. She most definitely was a *presence*. Kate felt invisible.

The woman came straight over to her. "Hi, I'm looking for an antique paperweight for a friend." She spoke with a deep Southern drawl.

"We've got a nice selection." Kate pulled out a display tray lined with black velvet. The woman reached over to pick up an antique baccarat millefiori. Her hands were beautifully manicured with bright red polish. In contrast, Kate's hands displayed chewed nails and torn cuticles. She put them down at her sides.

"This is awfully pretty." The woman was eyeing a Boston and Sandwich weight containing a purple poinsettia.

"Isn't it? But I love this Murano." Kate pointed to a weight with a large blue flower glowing in its interior. "It's magical."

The woman went back and forth and eventually chose the Murano. They chatted while Kate wrapped it up. After the woman left, Kate took out her sketch pad and began to draw, letting the designs flow on their own. It was a nautical theme with anchors and seagulls on a blue background with touches of red. She used colored pencils to fill in her initial design. This was very different from her usual subject matter. She must have seen something the other day when she took her lunch down to the wharf; something that had set her mind on this path. She was so engrossed in her work that she didn't hear Cyril come up behind her.

He peered over her shoulder. "Hey, I like that. It would make great wallpaper for a nautical-themed room." He picked up her sketch pad to look more closely. "Yes, that's nice." He flipped through the pages, raising it higher when she reached up to grab it back.

Kate felt exposed. She'd never shown her work to Cyril or Neil. "Cyril, don't. Don't look through my sketches, please.

He ignored her and kept turning pages. "Katherine, these are wonderful."

She clammed up, feeling stripped bare. Too many times in her life, people had made fun of her drawings. Her parents ripped up her sketches and told her to spend her time doing something useful like studying math or doing the breakfast dishes. Sam had always sneered at the sketches. "Do something productive, Kat. If you've got so much time to kill, go clean the toilets."

Cyril called out, "Neil, come look at these. Katherine has been hiding her talents from us."

Neil came clicking down the hall. He reached the counter and leaned on it. Cyril set down the sketch pad and slowly turned each page. "Look at these tiny flowers...exquisite. And these silky ribbons of color, they're flowing right down the page, perfect and intricate."

"This one with the little fish is fun. It would work for a kid's bedroom," Neil said.

They kept going right through the sketch pad, making comments. Kate watched feeling apprehensive. When they had finished, they both turned and faced her.

"You've got talent, baby. Yes, you do," Cyril whistled softly.

Neil hobbled over to his favorite armchair and sat down. It was for sale but Kate figured he liked it too much to ever sell it. "I think you could sell some of this stuff, Katherine. You've got a real flair."

"Really? You think so? I pretty much just draw for pleasure."

"Yes, I do. Cyril, why don't we contact Harry Stein? He would jump at this stuff. I can see wallpaper, tablecloths, stationery, cards. Hell, you could frame some of these."

"Yeah, they have a new fresh feeling that I haven't seen anywhere." Cyril handed back the sketch pad as if it were a priceless piece of antique china. "Katherine, my girl, you're going to be the next Laura Ashley."

Chapter 21   Cici

October, then

Cici's life had fallen into a pattern. She was at the bakery by five forty-five and opened up at six. Just like back home, she often had a cup of coffee and a croissant with André, and then he was off to bed. At eight Napoléon appeared after having done the deliveries to local hotels and restaurants. They worked through the day together serving customers and preparing pastries. Cici usually went home at four when André came back to see how the day had gone.

The first morning when she arrived in her new dress with its sprigs of flowers, André whistled and told her she looked too nice to work in his humble shop. Then she put on her crisp apron and he smiled with pleasure. "You are bringing a breath of fresh air. Customers will come flocking."

Cici spent a lot of time the first few weeks rearranging and polishing up the display cases; adding little touches, like doilies under some cakes and silver or gold-backed cardboard for other pastries. She had convinced André to spend some money on new display trays and some attractive glass and silver cake stands for the front window. On Craigslist she found a couple of small round wrought-iron tables with glass tops and matching chairs. Another expense was a new red, white and blue striped awning that gave a fresh zippy look to the store. The regulars like Monsieur Bernard complimented André on his new hire who was sprucing up the place. "Now the bread and pastries have always been the best, but let's face it, my man, you were letting this place fall apart. You needed Mademoiselle Cécile."

By October, traffic into the store had definitely increased. Tourists who would have walked right past were drawn into the clean, neat and ever-so-French atmosphere. An increase in business meant more work in the kitchens. André hired Carlos, a young Cuban kid who became his apprentice and worked nights. Carlos was a gifted young man, quick to learn.

At the end of her shift Cici sat at the little glass table and went over the day's sales with André. He was freshest then, after his day of sleeping, and most open to her suggestions. Lately they had been discussing the idea of offering small sandwiches at lunch time. "I envision small croissant sandwiches, you know, maybe shrimp or chicken salad." Cici said.

"Wouldn't that be a lot of extra work for you?"

"I think Napoléon and I could manage it after the morning rush. We often have people come in asking for something more substantial around noon."

"Hmm…maybe… if you could handle it?" André folded his arms and rested them on his protruding stomach. In front of him was a tall glass of iced coffee.

She was already thinking a mile a minute. "And how about ham or brie or pâté on a baguette…a little crispy green lettuce and a slice of bright tomato. Doesn't that sound yummy?" Cici had her eyes closed, envisioning the perfect sandwich.

"You are bringing a lot of changes, *mon amie*. I don't know if I can keep up with you."

Cici opened her eyes, worried. "I don't want to make things too difficult for you. Is all this too much? Just tell me."

"No, no. I've got to be ready to change." He stared out the window at the street, which had quieted down in the late afternoon. "When my Marie died, I stopped caring about the pâtisserie. I was, how do you say, going through the motions."

His gaze turned back to Cici's. "Now I feel regenerated. I feel better coming to work and making a go of it."

Cici's smiled with pleasure. "I'm so glad. We make a good team with Napoléon and Carlos."

"Yes, we do, with you as our Queen Bee." He looked down at his watch. "It's time you go home. You've been here almost twelve hours."

"*D'accord*, I'm out of here." She slipped on her mini backpack, blew kisses to André and headed out the door.

The walk home was always a pleasure after being in the shop all day. She was tired from being on her feet but enjoyed ambling along through the long rays of sunshine that dappled the sidewalk.

That morning a real jerk had come in at ten o'clock and yelled at her and Napoléon about his delivery. Apparently, he had not received the right number of croissants that morning. She checked the order catalogue and saw thirty items listed.

"I had a breakfast group booked today," the guy said. "Last week, I called and said to double my order. I ended up having to give these ladies whole wheat toast." The guy's face was mottled and he had his fists on his hips. If he calmed down he would have been kind of cute. He had a blond ponytail and looked more like a surfer than a chef.

Cici ran her finger up and down the orders in the book. "I don't see...wait a minute...I've got a double order written here for tomorrow. It's the Sunrise Café, right?" She looked up at him under her shock of blond bangs.

The guy was studying her. "How long have you worked here? I don't remember you."

"I've been here since September. But sir, I'm the one who took this order and I remember you said it was on Veteran's Day that you wanted a double order. That's tomorrow."

"I did?" He was still looking at her, distracted.

80

"Yes, you did," Cici said with finality.

He let out a breath and visibly calmed down. "Well, I guess I screwed up. That doesn't happen too often."

"Maybe you're not as perfect as you might think." Cici closed the book with a snap. The guy had annoyed her. "Anyway, I'm sorry about the mix-up. How can we make it up to you?"

He looked her up and down. "Maybe you could do the delivery next time?"

Cici just shook her head at him and slipped through the curtain into the back of the shop, leaving Napoléon to deal with their unhappy customer.

By her front gate, she opened the wooden mailbox and found a letter from home. Her mother still preferred snail mail and Cici looked forward to her letters. She opened the gate and then stopped short. Sitting on the porch in the shade was a dog, a golden retriever.

"How did you get in here?" she said. The dog stood up and wagged its tail.

Cici went up the steps. "Did you get stuck in here? Come on, I'll let you out of the yard." She beckoned to the dog and went back down the steps. The dog didn't follow. She went back up and reached down gingerly for its collar. The dog licked her hand. Cici gave it a pat, then took hold of the collar and pulled the dog down the stairs and out through the gate. It followed along obediently.

"There you go." She patted the dog on the head again and went back inside the yard, shutting the gate firmly behind her. By the time she reached her door, the dog had cleared the fence and trotted back up the porch stairs. It waited expectantly while she opened the door.

Cici sighed. This was the last thing she needed at the end of a really long day. She was going to have to find the dog's owner. "What's your name, boy?" The dog considered her, its head cocked to the side. It really was a beautiful dog. It looked well cared for, with soft silky fur.

Cici crouched down and took hold of the collar, turning it to look for a tag. On the underside she found a small cylinder that was just the right size to hold a mini Chinese scroll.

"Wow, you're a mystery dog with a secret message." She tried to open the cylinder but both ends were stuck shut. The dog sat patiently gazing at Cici. She decided to take the collar off. Once it was removed, the dog shook itself all over. "I bet that feels good, right?" She couldn't believe she was having this one-sided conversation with a dog.

Cici went inside and into the kitchen, and put the collar on the counter. The dog followed her and stood looking expectant. "I bet you're thirsty, right?" Cici took out an old metal bowl and filled it with water. She put it down and the dog began lapping up the water.

Cici took a fork to the cylinder and succeeded in prying off one end. Using her fingernail, she managed to extract a piece of paper rolled into a tight spiral. She reached down and patted the dog, and then spread out the note on the kitchen counter. The dog sat down, wagging its tail.

The note said, *Hello. Please take care of Brandy for me. I can't keep her. I'm leaving town. She's had her shots and she's trained to walk without a leash. You'll love her. I do. Thank you.*

Cici looked down at her new friend and sighed. Could she take on the responsibility of a dog? Did she want to? She went over to the sofa and sat down, the note in one hand. Brandy came over and sniffed the note. Then she leaned against Cici's leg and put her head in Cici's lap. She looked up, her eyes limpid pools of love. Cici was hooked.

Chapter 22   Kate
January, now

Kate was stretched out on the sofa in Dr. Zuckerman's office. Covered with the baby blue blanket, she felt as though she were wrapped in a cocoon of warmth and safety. This was the norm now, once a week. She was here, lying on the sofa, nice and warm but it wasn't always so good. Sometimes when she remembered a difficult time in the past, she would shiver uncontrollably as if Arctic air had seeped into her bones.

Dr. Leah picked up her pad and paper. "What shall we talk about today?"

"I don't know. What do you think?" In her heart of hearts Kate always wanted to please. She was trying to think what would make the psychologist happy. But Dr. Leah didn't play her game. There was a long, pregnant silence. Pregnant, yes. To what memory would she give birth? More silence. An image of her father came to mind.

"I don't really look like my mother or my father. He was blond, large and hefty, a football player. He lost his hair quite early and would comb the few strands left across the top of his pink scalp. His eyes were blue. That Nordic blue, you know? Always cold and demanding."

"My mother was dark and thin. She was a traditional homemaker who never worked outside the house. Every night before my father came home she would change into a pretty dress and they would have cocktails in the living room.

"We had dinner at the dining-room table with crystal, china and candles in tall silver candelabra. My mother came from money. She held the purse strings but not always the power."

Silence.

"No one knows where my red hair came from," Kate said.

"Red hair?" Dr. Leah said, her eyebrows raised.

She hadn't wanted to reveal that fact. "Yes. I'm really a redhead but I need to have black hair. I need to be dark and black. Everyone notices red hair."

Dr. Leah crossed her legs, but said nothing.

"I was always a disappointment. I wasn't good at sports and my dad was a coach…a college football coach. He really wanted a boy and he pushed me into soccer, softball, basketball, but I wasn't good at anything." More images filled her mind and the words flowed out of her. Dr. Zuckerman listened with an interested gaze, but without showing any emotion.

"My mother wanted me to play the piano. She played the harp. I remember lying in bed at night, hearing the soft cascading notes wafting up to my bedroom. She entertained people at the hospital in the cancer center. Her music brought them solace." Kate squeezed the edges of the blanket. She closed her eyes, wishing away the unbidden memories.

"I was terrible at the piano. Once I was in a piano recital. I got up on the stage and sat down at the bench but I couldn't remember how the piece went. My mind went blank. I just sat there surrounded by this terrible silence. Finally, my piano teacher came and led me off the stage." She twisted the corner of the blanket in a tight knot.

"After the recital we were supposed to go out for dinner but my dad was so angry that he just drove us home. I sat in the back of the car feeling his anger roll over me like molten lava. At home he sent me to the piano in the living room and told me to practice for two hours. Then he left and went to the golf course bar. My mother hid in the kitchen behind the swinging door and I sat at the piano playing the recital piece over and over. It came back to my mind and my fingers." Kate pressed her palms against her eyes, seeing the darkened living room again, remembering that feeling of hopelessness.

"Are your parents still alive?" Dr. Zuckerman's voice was low.

"No, my dad died about two years ago. My mom, she had Alzheimer's. She was in a home for several years and died last summer."

"So now you're alone."

"Yes, I guess I'm an orphan. Can you be an orphan when you're an adult?" She paused, clasping her hands together. "I almost think this is better for me. No one is left to criticize me. ... I do a good job of that myself."

Chapter 23 Cici
November, then

Cici brought Brandy to work on a regular basis. She put a mat outside by the front door with a bowl of water. Brandy spent her time in the shade or behind the bakery out of view. The dog made lots of local friends and seemed unperturbed by other dogs that walked by.

Every day after the lunch crunch, Cici took Brandy for a brisk walk. At four o'clock they took the long way home and sometimes ended up at the Higgs Beach dog park so Brandy could have a romp with some of her canine buddies.

At home, Cici took a dip in the small pool which didn't allow for strenuous swimming but was cool and inviting. When she got out she fluffed her hair and wrapped up in a white terrycloth robe. With a glass of chilled wine in hand, she went into the library alcove.

After work was the most emotionally stressful time of the day. When she was busy at the pâtisserie, she didn't have time to think. But as shadows lengthened in the late afternoon, Cici felt the dark guilt fill her mind. At first she tried to stay busy cleaning or cooking something elaborate for herself. When those activities didn't give her relief, she turned to her journal.

She'd kept one ever since the accident. It was cathartic to hash out her feelings on paper. She'd had a diary as a teenager, a red leather-bound book Oscar had given her for her fourteenth birthday. She'd brought it with her to Key West and tucked it on a shelf in the library alcove. Back then, she'd wanted to be a cheerleader and had a crush on a boy named Connor O'Keefe. Reading those pages, she had a sense of love and pity for her former self. It struck her that life was never easy. Now, in the alcove with pen in hand, she filled pages of a spiral bound notebook with her careful script.

Some nights Cici rewrote history. What if Myra Wilkins hadn't called her down to the office that February afternoon? What if she had left at three o'clock with everyone else? The accident wouldn't have happened. She would have gone to the bar to meet the other teachers and she would have fallen in love with Jeremy and she would be happily married now and gainfully employed at Lakeland High School.

Little Betsy Tripp's mother would have noticed that her daughter wasn't in the house. She would have gone out into the blizzard and brought her little girl home. Betsy would have spent that night safe in bed wearing Dora the Explorer pajamas. Now, ten months later, she would be in preschool and running across the playground, giggling with her friends, strawberry blond curls flying out behind her.

Other times Cici imagined that when the paramedics came, they had revived Betsy. She wasn't dead, just had a few bruises. She would rub her eyes and smile at Cici. Then the two of them would go into the house for a cup of hot chocolate.

Some nights she wrote stories of reincarnation. Betsy was reborn exactly the same. Her parents were so happy to have their little girl back. Scientists talked about a miracle.

One night she wrote a fairy tale about a little girl who saved the world. The dragon of the North swept down bringing winter and cold to the land. He was angry because he had never experienced the warmth of love. Each swipe of his tail brought ice and snow. Icy crystals covered the trees. Birds were frozen in flight. Only a little child could save the land…a girl who was innocent and pure. This child wasn't afraid and went out and blew warm kisses at the dragon and showered him with words of love. In return the dragon blew fire from his mouth and warmed the world. Soon flowers were growing and happiness reigned.

Sometimes, thoughts of Betsy's parents and brother appeared unbidden. Cici had never met the mother. Only the father had appeared in court. Cici was found not guilty of involuntary manslaughter due to the blizzard conditions and the snowdrift that concealed the small child sitting in the street. Mr. Tripp had barely acknowledged Cici's presence. She had feared the parents' animosity towards her, but Betsy's father seemed to hold his wife responsible. "She wasn't watching our kid. She was upstairs, banging on the computer," he'd said.

Cici could imagine the pain the mother felt. She wondered how the woman was doing now. Was she able to sleep? Could she ever forget? Did she hate Cici with a vengeance?

One evening, her journal laid aside for the moment, Cici scrolled through the online site of the *Keynoter* newspaper. The lead article in the Living and Entertainment section was about the 23rd annual Schooner Wharf Minimal Regatta. The vessels had to be made out of plywood, duct tape and two-by-fours. Apparently any craft that could float won a prize. The picture was pretty funny.

She clicked on the classifieds next, to check out apartments for rent. She'd been toying with the idea of getting a roommate. Apart from the company, she could use a little more cash to manage expenses. Her salary wasn't much and she was just making it. She decided to give Oscar a call.

Oscar sounded upbeat when he answered. "How's it going, *ma poulette*?"

She didn't want to talk about the loneliness that sometimes overwhelmed her. "I'm thinking about getting a roommate," she said. "What do you think?"

"Hold on, let me just get these baguettes in their trays."

She could hear the fans. Oscar must be downstairs near the ovens. When he came back on the line, she continued. "I was thinking I'd like some company and that a little more money would be nice. Would that be all right with you?"

"*Ecoute*, Cécile, consider that house your own. If you want a roommate, that's fine by me. But if you're having trouble money-wise, we could help out."

"No, no, no. I'm fine. Don't you and Maman worry. I am *not* asking for money." The last thing she wanted was to have them sending her a stipend. They had already done so much for her.

"Okay, okay. So, you just want my opinion? I think it sounds like a good idea. Just be careful who you get. Why don't you call Robert Smith? I used to have him rent the cottage for me. He's a really nice guy. Give him a call and he'll help you vet the applicants. Tell him I gave you his name."

"Robert Smith?"

"Oui, it's the *Smith and Smith Realty Company*."

After she hung up, Cici clicked on to Craigslist for the Florida Keys. She planned to furnish the second bedroom with the basics. It would be fun to paint the room and decorate.

Chapter 24   Kate

January, now

Today, Dr. Leah was wearing a pretty yellow dress that would look great at a garden party if she ever attended one. It highlighted her tawny skin. Kate felt pallid in comparison. Today she'd brought a grey cardigan to wear in the office. She lay back against the sofa cushions and closed her eyes as Dr. Leah spoke.

"You said you got divorced last May. What happened after that? How did that make you feel?"

"After the divorce, I moved back to the college town where I grew up. I didn't know where else to go. I'd never lived alone and my parents' house was empty. Bessie, the cleaning woman we'd had for years, came by once a week to check on things."

"Where were your parents?"

"My father had moved my mother into a nursing home several years before that specialized in Alzheimer's patients. At first he tried to take care of her himself. That surprised me. He was so gentle, so concerned." She looked over at Leah, who merely nodded her head.

"He was so kind and so patient. He'd never been like that before, certainly not with me. He truly loved her, I guess. But as the disease progressed, Mother's behavior became more erratic. My father kept the doors locked and had an aide come in to help. But several times Mother escaped and wandered the streets at night. One time she was nearly killed. So he made the big decision to institutionalize her."

"What about your father? Dealing with a loved one with Alzheimer's can be debilitating."

"After my mother was settled in the home, my father became a recluse. At first he visited her every day and then played golf or hung out at the college where he was still welcome in the football locker room. But gradually he stopped going anywhere. I got calls from neighbors about the condition of the house and the yard. I telephoned him but half the time he wouldn't pick up. When he did, he told me to mind my own business. I went down there a couple of times with the kids, but they made him nervous. I never could get Sam to go with me, and Sam was the person my father wanted most to see…" The thought of Sam made her face grow warm. She didn't want to talk about him.

"In retrospect I was naïve. My father was one of those men who seems tough and independent, but whose strength actually comes from the woman he loves. Without my mother to share his life, he lost the will to live. He died a year later of a heart attack. Bessie found him upstairs in bed, my mother's picture in his hands." She clasped her hands together over her chest. There was a long moment of silence.

"So after the divorce you went home to live in an empty house?" Leah prompted.

"Yes. I took a bus from Chicago and then a taxi. Sam kept the cars when he told me to get out. Everything was in his name…" Her voice had taken on a dreamy quality as though she were hypnotized. "It was pouring when I got out of the taxi, so I ran for the porch. I remember fumbling with the lock; I was so drenched…" She took a deep breath. "When I stepped into the foyer I expected to hear Mother's voice, or Father's cough. It was so quiet. Eerie. I could feel the house vibrating with voices from the past. I went from room to room listening to the familiar creaks of the floorboards. Bessie had kept things clean, but the furniture looked tired and shabby. In the entryway and up the stairs, the carpeting was threadbare. In the living room the flowered sateen sofa my mother loved was shiny with age and the coffee table had deep scratches. They had this sixties-type kitchen, an avocado-colored refrigerator and orange and green wallpaper. It all looked old and tired."

She heard the rustle of fabric as Dr. Leah crossed her legs. The outpouring of memories went on; as if the doctor's quiet presence had unlocked a door.

"Upstairs, my old bedroom had been turned into an office. So I settled in the guest room. Frilly bedspread, lace curtains. The shades were drawn throughout the house. It felt like a damp cocoon. Rain pounded on the roof. I remember pulling off my clothes and getting under the covers. I spent two days like that…in bed. I think it rained the whole time. Time slipped by me, washed away with the rain and my tears." Kate's voice was hollow.

"You must have been very unhappy." Leah said softly.

"I couldn't face myself… what I had lost…the life I'd destroyed. I don't know why I didn't kill myself." Her eyes flew open, her gaze unfocused.

"Bessie came and found me. I was dehydrated and starving. She brought me downstairs and made me chicken soup. In a way she brought me back to life. She stayed for a couple of weeks and cared for me like a baby. At first I spent long hours on the back porch just watching the birds. Then I started working in the garden, pulling weeds and planting stuff. Working in the dirt with my hands was therapeutic."

Still Dr. Leah said nothing. Kate kept talking, her own voice lulling her into a trance-like state, seeing the past more clearly than the room where she lay. "I did the same things every day. In the morning I walked to the nursing home to visit my mother. She was always sitting in the sun on the veranda, in her wheelchair, talking to herself or telling the caregivers what to do. She called them all Katherine. 'Katherine, you better clean your room. Go upstairs right now and get to work.' 'Katherine, lower your voice. Remember, a loud voice bespeaks a vacant mind.' 'Have you practiced the piano? You better get in there now.'

"It didn't matter who was nearby, man or woman. She always called them Katherine." Kate chuckled. "The funny thing was she never recognized me when I sat down right next to her. Can you believe it? She would say, 'Who are you? Don't sit so close to me.' And scrunch her face up with disdain."

"Relating to someone with Alzheimer's disease is very difficult."

Kate rubbed her face with her hands. "Towards the end of June, Mother came down with pneumonia and they moved her to the hospital. It all happened so fast. She was only there a few days and then she was gone. I had never satisfied her. I was always a disappointment." Tears trickled out from between her fingers. "Then I was truly alone."

Chapter 25 Cici
November, then

Cici and Napoléon were making sandwiches. It was ten o'clock and the bakery was quiet. She opened the refrigerated display case and placed a tray of shrimp salad croissants on the top shelf. They had been laughing about their latest customer, Henry Sanders. Mr. Sanders was retired and came in for a mocha-chocolate éclair every morning. They knew for a fact that his wife kept him on a strict diet at home, which was why he sneaked in for his mid-morning pastry. He usually sat at one of the little tables and chatted with them while he ate it. The fact that he was diabetic made Cici feel a little guilty about serving him his prohibited treat, but she wasn't certain about telling him "no" either.

"I think he's lonely and comes here for company as well as a forbidden snack," Cici said.

"*D'accord*, but the éclair, it is not so good for him."

"Can we deny a customer what he wants?"

"In a bar, they will stop serving you if you're drunk."

"You're right. But I don't have the heart to deny him his small pleasure. I mean, I don't want to be Big Brother watching him." Cici looked up and saw Mr. Sunrise Café outside on the sidewalk, patting Brandy. The dog lay on her back in total abandon. Brandy had no discriminating taste and seemed happy to let this jerk scratch her tummy.

Just as that thought crossed Cici's mind, Mr. Sunrise Café looked up and waved at her from the doorway. "Hello. Where did this retriever come from? I don't remember seeing a dog the last time I was here."

Cici rolled her eyes. "The last time you were here, you wouldn't have noticed an elephant by the front door."

Mr. Sunrise Café didn't respond. He walked in and surveyed the sandwich display. "Those look good." He came over to the counter. Cici kept her back to him as she cut open a baguette. "Hey, I just stopped by to say my customers love the new almond and apricot croissants. They're a big hit."

"These are Mademoiselle Cécile's addition. She has many new ideas," Napoléon said.

Cici didn't turn around. She carefully arranged a ham slice on the bread.

"And I wanted to say I'm sorry about the other day."

Still with her back to him, Cici said, "No problem."

"So is that your dog?"

"Yes, that's Brandy. She's a rescue dog." She arranged some cheese slices on the ham.

A customer came in. Cici turned around, all smiles. "Can I help you?"

"A loaf of the country bread and two lemon tarts, please. The woman had a sunburn almost as pink as her sundress and flip flops. She was probably a tourist down for a few days of sun. They often overdid it. "Oh, and could I have two slices of the praline torte? It looks so good."

"Certainly." Cici put the pastries in a box with the bakery logo on it and wrapped up the bread.

The customer turned to Mr. Sunrise Café. "Isn't this a nice place?"

"It certainly is. The employees are so friendly and sweet." He smiled at Cici, who frowned at him.

The woman paid and left the shop with her purchases. Napoléon slipped through the curtain to the back. A vibrating silence filled the room.

"So my café closes at three PM." He put both hands on the counter.

"That's nice."

"What time do you leave here?"

"Me? I go home between four and five. Why?"

"I'd like you to have dinner with me." He stood there smiling at her. She noticed the fine blond hair on his arms and legs. He wore khaki shorts and a blue polo shirt that set off his blue eyes.

"I don't know…"

"You don't know if you want to have dinner?"

"I don't know *you*. I don't even know your name."

"I'm Bryan with a 'y'. What's your name?"

"I'm Cécile with an *accent aigue*." She gave the last two words a French pronunciation.

He looked mystified.

"Bryan, why do you want to have dinner with me?"

"Cécile, I like your spicy personality…and besides, I think you're cute."

Cici rolled her eyes. "We might not have anything to say to each other. It could be a very long dinner."

"Let's try. How about I pick you up at six o'clock?"

"Well…"

"Be adventuresome. Take a chance on me."

"Well…"

"We can bring Brandy if you want. I was thinking about The Afterdeck Bar. You can bring dogs there."

"Well…okay."

Cici told him where she lived on Olivia Street. After Bryan left she felt warmth bubbling up from deep down inside.

Chapter 26   Leah
January, now

Katherine lay under the blue blanket, her eyes closed. She and Leah were having their usual unvoiced standoff. Leah smiled. "Katherine, what would you like to talk about?"

"I don't know. I feel so tired today."

More silence. Leah smoothed her skirt.

"I could talk about my husband, my ex-husband," Katherine said. "But I don't know if I can."

Silence. Leah saw a flush creeping up Katherine's face. "Go on."

"I met him when I was a freshman in college. He was a junior and had just transferred in that fall. My dad was thrilled because Sam was a quarterback and he was going to make all the difference to the team."

She picked at the blanket, her gaze roving around the room. Then she closed her eyes. "The first time I met him was at the barbeque my parents always held at the beginning of the school year. They invited all the football players to our house. I remember my dad brought Sam over to introduce me. Sam was the son my father never had. They even looked alike."

She opened her eyes and stared up at the ceiling.

"The second time I met him was in the student cafeteria. I was getting a cup of coffee and he came up behind me and put his hands on my shoulders. He was a big guy with big hands. I remember the weight of them, pressing me down. He kind of spun me around and led me over to the booth where he was sitting. I sat down across from him. He asked me a bunch of questions. It was like an interview. Then he talked a lot about himself. He always did that. I just sat there obediently. I knew my father would want me to be nice to this prize catch."

Katherine looked up at Dr. Leah. "Not only was Sam the best quarterback that little school had ever had, but he was also a good student. He attacked everything with the same compulsion. Nothing held him back from what he wanted. In his favor, he pushed himself to the limits." Her hands were clenched and she took a deep breath. "Sam was adopted, but he abandoned his parents when he was eighteen. I don't know why. He never mentioned them and I never met them."

Leah nodded. Katherine was growing agitated, clutching the edge of the blanket. They might have to pull the plug on this session before too much longer.

Katherine took a deep breath and shut her eyes tight. "The third time I met him, he came to our house for dinner. My mother went all out with steak, twice-baked potatoes, salad, garlic bread, lemon meringue pie. That was her specialty. I remember it all. That night is etched in my brain." She turned her head back and forth on the pillow. "I helped her prepare everything. I lived at home, not in the dorms. It was cheaper that way."

Her voice took on a robotic note. "After dinner my parents left for a reception at the home of the college president. They left Sam and me alone. I tried to start a conversation but he wasn't interested. He headed into my dad's study where the whiskey was kept. I don't know how he knew that, but he did. He took a drink right out of the bottle and asked me if I wanted some. I said no and then he drank some more. I just stood in the middle of the room feeling guilty. I never went into my dad's study, especially when he wasn't there."

"Sam came over and pulled me down onto the leather sofa. He started kissing me. I had never dated. I didn't know what to do. Nobody had ever kissed me like that. And then he opened my blouse and he kept kissing me and he tasted like garlic and whiskey and he touched my breast and I didn't do anything. And then he reached down under my skirt, touching my underpants. And he said, 'Are you a redhead down there. That will be a first for me.' And then he pulled off my underpants, telling me to bring up my legs so he could get them off, and I did."

Katherine's eyes were open but Leah could tell she wasn't in the doctor's office. She was back in her father's study. "He unzipped his pants and was on top of me." She shuddered. "He raped me, right there, on the leather sofa, in my dad's study and I didn't do anything. I just lay there. Just like I did over and over and over during all of my marriage."

She yanked the blanket off and stood up, knocking into the low table. Voice rising and eyes wild, she paced back and forth across the room. "I never did anything. I always just lay there. I hate him. I really hate him." Her body shook with anger. Then she looked directly at Leah. "But I also hate *me*... for what *I* let him do to *me*."

Chapter 27 Cici

November, then

Cici and Bryan went to Louis's Backyard at the Afterdeck Bar with Brandy in tow. Seeing as how they'd first met when he came into the bakery to complain, Cici thought she would feel uncomfortable with him, but instead she soon felt as though they'd been friends forever. She couldn't explain it.

Cici had on a pink sheath and sandals. Bryan looked preppy in a pressed shirt and dark dress pants. They definitely looked like a first-date couple. He had a vintage Ford convertible and there was plenty of room for Brandy in the back seat.

"What a fun car. What year is it?" Cici asked.

"1962. What do you drive?"

"I don't have a car. I don't really need one."

"But you do know how to drive, right?"

"Yes." Cici didn't want to say she would never drive again. She changed the subject. "Where did you grow up?"

"Right here. I'm a home-grown boy."

"So you don't even know what it's like to be cold?"

"I guess I don't. When I was a kid I always wanted to play in the snow but it never happened. Now I'm too busy to leave."

"You're not missing anything. I am *so* happy to be out of all that." She shivered, pulling her white pashmina around her shoulders.

When they arrived at the restaurant they learned that dogs were only allowed before five PM. "I should have checked this out. I'm so sorry," Bryan said.

"Hey, that's fine. Let's drop Brandy off at home. We can come back here or go somewhere else," Cici said.

"No way. I promised Brandy was going to be part of the party!" He paused, then said, "Listen. How about I make dinner for you at the restaurant? Brandy could wander around the garden area. It's enclosed."

"Do you really want to do that? That's what you do all day long."

He looked over smiling. "It would be fun to cook for you. I can woo you with my culinary skills."

"Maybe I could help. Toss the salad or stir the soup." She smiled back.

Cici had never seen The Sunrise Café. It was on a corner with a lattice-covered patio off to one side. The exterior was painted royal blue, pink, purple and orange, a typical Key West color scheme. Bryan unlocked the door and they went in. He flipped a switch and a series of lights came on. Meriden blue pendant lights hung low over white-clothed tables. Colorful napkins and sparkling silver made up the table settings.

Bryan picked up two wine glasses and headed to the bar at the back of the room. "How about a glass of wine? I've got this Argentinian Malbec that's really good. I think you'll like it…very smooth."

Cici didn't really know her wines although she had been brought up with a bottle on the table every night. She nodded. "I'd love to try it."

Their dinner was simple but delicious. While she perched on a stool, he made them a salad with julienned beets, goat cheese and walnuts on a bed of lettuce. The dressing was a little bit of this and little bit of that…champagne vinegar, walnut oil, mustard and a mysterious mix of herbs. Then he made a mushroom, asparagus and gruyère omelet. It was all served on the most beautiful dishes Cici had ever seen; china painted with waves of blue, turquoise and purple.

They decided to eat on the patio. Bryan placed several votive candles and an orchid on their table. Then he carried out four plates balanced on his hands and arms while Cici brought their glasses of wine. They sat down and dug in.

"Mmm, this is so good," Cici said, enjoying a bite of the omelet.

"Here's the bread from my favorite bakery." He passed her a wicker basket.

Cici helped herself. "So what was it like growing up in Key West?"

"Lots of fishing, lots of swimming, lots of running around with friends, and complete disdain for tourists. I mean, we resented all these people coming down here from up north. Of course now they're a major part of my bread and butter."

"I can see how you would feel that way. But Key West lives off the tourists. I'm a neophyte so I like meeting all these people. Gosh, I'm almost one of them."

"I've changed my tune. I know this restaurant couldn't make it without the snowbirds."

"How did you get into this business?" Cici took a bite of the salad. It was delicious.

"This place belongs to my uncle, or let's say my uncle and me. I'm paying him off little by little. He didn't want to run it anymore and I offered to buy him out." He swirled the wine in his glass looking at it intently.

"But how did you become a cook?"

"I've always been interested in cooking. I used to hang out here as a kid. I learned a lot just watching my uncle. Then I went to Charleston to culinary school."

"What did your dad do? Was he into cooking too?"

Bryan looked up at her. "My parents were killed in a car accident when I was a little kid. They were just twenty-two and were speeding on the A1A. I don't really remember them..."

102

"That must have been hard." Her voice was low and sympathetic. The mention of a car accident had sent a shiver up her spine.

"So my aunt and uncle raised me."

"Where are they now?"

"My uncle works with my cousin who owns a couple of fishing boats that he charters. He spends most of his time out on the water. My aunt is here in town. Now that I run the restaurant, she's retired. I usually see them a couple of times a week. They come in for breakfast or I go over to the house for dinner. Their son is like a brother to me." He grinned at her.

"Wow, I know your life history." She looked down at her plate, which was almost empty. Bryan had been talking while she was eating.

"What about you? Tell me about your life." He began to eat his omelet.

Cici felt apprehensive. How much did she want to tell him? Even though she had changed her name, she worried that he could Google her and learn about the accident.

"I learned to bake by living over a bakery. My dad died when I was little, too...from cancer. My mom continued running the store with the help of a friend."

"Where are we talking about? New York?"

Her answer was clipped. "No. Chicago."

"Did you go to college?" He speared a piece of beet.

"Yes, I studied English literature."

"You didn't want to do something with that? Journalism or teaching?"

Cici sipped her wine, choosing her words. "I do like to write. I have a journal I write in every evening, but that isn't a career." She skipped the period when she was teaching. He didn't need to know everything about her. "Anyway, this friend of my mother knows André Guérin, who owns the Pâtisserie-

Boulangerie down here. André needed some help since his wife died so I came down."

"Are you going to stick around? Or are you here temporarily for a change of scene?" His expression was sincere.

She avoided looking into his eyes. "I don't know."

He grinned at her. "I hope you decide to stick around."

Chapter 28   Kate
February, now

Harry Stein was coming into town. Cyril and Neil were taking him out for lunch to Blue Heaven. Harry was an old friend from back in California when they all lived in Laguna Beach. Now he lived in L. A. and his interior design business was booming. He had jumped into the international world of household fabrics and wall coverings.

They had encouraged Kate to come as well. They wanted to introduce her and use the occasion to present her drawings.

"Wear something feminine, maybe a little color," Neil had suggested gently.

She got the message. She'd gone shopping and bought an outfit, though it seemed like a crazy expense considering she'd only wear it once.

The afternoon before the luncheon was exhausting. At her shrink session, she had divulged her life with Sam and the rape...the first rape. Somehow, expressing the terrific anger she'd felt had been liberating. She'd never allowed herself to face what happened, but by telling it all to Dr. Leah, she felt as if the burden had been partially lifted.

"I let everyone tell me what to do, how to live, how to think," she'd said at the end of the session, after she calmed down. "I don't know if I can change overnight. But I'm going to try to be stronger and stand up for myself."

Dr. Leah had smiled. "That you've acknowledged this to yourself is half the battle. I'm proud of you today. You're on the right path."

At home she had lain on the bed clutching her locket in one hand and pressing Timmy's picture to her heart. She'd gotten another letter from Sam, but stuffed it in the desk drawer without opening it. Why did he still write to her? He was still pulling the strings from afar, ranting at her or telling her she would never see Timmy again. Would she ever be able to fight him for a place in Timmy's life?

When she walked into the shop at noon, Neil and Cyril were bowled over. They had never seen her in anything but her black garb. Today she wore a sea green silk cheongsam, hip-length with frog closures, and white linen pants. Her earrings were swirls of green and turquoise shaped like pearls. She'd put on make-up and done her hair in a smooth bun at the nape of her neck.

"You are exquisite, my dear," Neil said.

"Yep, all the heads will turn when we get to the restaurant," Cyril added.

For the first time in years, Kate felt alluring. For too long, she'd been told she was overweight and unattractive. She couldn't help beaming at her two gentlemen admirers.

Cyril opened the door with a flourish. "Your chariot awaits."

They drove to Blue Heaven in Bahama Village. The place had a lot of local color and was a favorite of Harry's when he visited. Kate didn't know what Cyril had told Harry but he seemed surprised by her appearance. They had probably mentioned what a miserable sad sack she was, always dressed in mourning.

Harry was bald with dark deep-set eyes in an ascetic face. He was slim but gave an impression of strength. His handshake was brief and intense.

They were seated under a canopy of tropical foliage, Kate placed next to Harry. They all started with a *caipirinha*, a Brazilian rum drink. Kate hadn't drunk alcohol since moving to Key West. The rum went right to her head and turned her

106

cheeks rosy. When Neil told her how pretty she looked, she blushed and stared down at the table.

For lunch, all three men had the loaded black bean bowl with corn bread, which looked delectable. Kate selected a shrimp Caesar salad. She ate slowly, enjoying every bite and letting the laughter and reminisces spill over her. When the coffee came, Neil suggested that Kate bring out her drawings, which she'd brought in a portfolio carrying case. Shyly, she handed the portfolio to Harry Stein. He cleared a space in front of him and undid the ribbons. Kate felt her heart doing flip flops in her chest.

He spent a long time looking at each page. Then he went back and considered them again. She couldn't tell from his face what he was thinking. They all watched Harry as if suspended in time. Kate realized she'd been holding her breath.

She'd promised herself she would be more assertive. Why not start now? She sat up straight and leaned slightly forward. "Tell me Mr. Stein. What do you think of my work?"

He considered her over the top of his reading glasses. "I think they're marvelous. Yes, marvelous. Very fresh, very vibrant. You've got a lot of talent."

For the second time that day, Kate blushed. This time she wasn't going to sink into her seat. "Really? I'm thrilled." She took a deep breath. "Would you like to use them?"

She caught Cyril and Neil exchanging a glance. Harry smiled at her.

"I would. I could probably take some of these and have my graphic artists work with them, but I need you to start working digitally. Have you worked with designing software?"

"I have in the past but not recently. I don't have a computer."

He looked at her as if she were an alien. "No computer?"

"Not currently, but I'll buy one and start working for you. I've used CorelDRAW and PainterX3 in the past." She looked at him, passion filling her eyes.

"All that sounds good. If you'll allow me to take some of your work, I'll draw up a contract and email it to you." He frowned. "Hang on. No computer, no email?"

"No sir, but I'll be up and running in a day or two."

Cyril and Neil beamed at each other. She guessed what they were thinking. Their protégé's career was taking off.

Chapter 29   Leah
February, now

Katherine wasn't lying under the blanket today. She was
sitting up and nervously curling a strand of hair with her
fingers. She had come in that morning looking like a different
person. There was a little color in her cheeks and she walked
with more self-confidence, not her usual slouch. Could all this
be due to the last session where she had faced some of her
demons?

"You seem upbeat today." Leah had said, smiling.

Katherine smiled back with a twinkle in her eye. "I'm
excited. I haven't been excited about anything for so long.
I've got a contract with this big interior design company. It's
called *Stein Design*. The owner is a friend of the guys I work
for. Mr. Stein came out here and looked at some of my work.
He liked it and he offered me a year's contract."

"Wow. That's great news!"

"To say I'm elated is an understatement. I'm going to
be paid for doing what I love. Isn't that cool?"

"Very cool. I'm happy to see you're having positive
feelings about yourself."

Katherine beamed at her; no feigning, no holding back.
*She has a lovely smile. She's actually a beautiful
woman,* Leah thought. Katherine's inner glow showed in her
face and in the way she held her body.

"So I probably should get to work here, right?"
Katherine said. She took off her sandals and lay down on the
sofa.

Leah removed a piece of fluff from the skirt of her
black linen dress. Silence prevailed as Katherine took a

moment to calm down and concentrate. "Should I talk more about Sam?"

"If you feel you need to…"

Her face lost its glow. "I married him to make my parents happy. My dad thought Sam walked on water and my mother was bewitched by his manners and charm. He *could* be charming.

"We had a great big wedding when he graduated. I had only two years of college. I meant to continue after the wedding. But then we moved to Chicago and I got pregnant. So I never finished school. First Timmy came along and then Betsy two years later." Katherine had definitely switched gears. Her exuberance when she'd walked in was gone. Her voice had taken on its usual robotic cadence.

"Does that bother you?"

"Yes, sometimes it does. I feel like a loser because I didn't push myself to take classes and finish. I guess I don't have any excuse. Most of the time I was alone with the kids because Sam was working his way up in the company and had to travel a lot. I always felt too tired to take on anything more."

Katherine continued to talk about the early days of her marriage and her husband's aggressive behavior. "Sam was very critical about how I raised the children. He didn't want Timmy to be coddled. When he was home he demanded strict discipline and would hit Timmy with a belt when he didn't mind. He could be very cruel verbally…to me and to Timmy."

"What about Betsy?" Leah said quietly after a small silence.

"Betsy? She was his little princess."

Silence fell again. Leah waited, sensing there was more.

"Timmy was easily frightened and needed a night-light for monsters and ghosts. Betsy wasn't afraid of anything. That's what Sam liked about her." Katherine's voice wavered.

More silence.

"I loved her too," Katherine said. "I loved her so much." Her voice was barely audible. Tears had begun to flow from her tightly closed eyes. She brought her hands to her face and sobbed, her shoulders shaking.

Leah felt her pain. Clearly something terrible had happened to her children but Katherine wasn't ready to talk about it. It was still locked up tight inside her. That night on the steps of the office building she had said the locket was all she had of Betsy.

"Do you want to talk about Betsy and what happened to her?"

Katherine reached for a Kleenex from the box on the table. "I can't. You'll hate me."

"That's not the issue here, Katherine. I won't hate you. But you have to learn to not hate yourself. That *is* the issue."

"I don't know. You're right. But I don't want to face that today. I can't talk about Betsy today." Slowly she sat up, clasping her hands in her lap and crossing her ankles.

"Well, we'll stop for today." Leah stood up and went to the computer to check her calendar. "Let's see, you're scheduled for Friday. Is that good?"

"I'll be here. I've got a lot to do now. I've got my job at the shop, designing and drawing, *and* I have to find a place to live."

"What do you mean?"

"They posted a sign at my place six weeks ago telling us we had to move out. The management sold the building. I haven't found another place I like that I can afford."

Leah was thinking. What had Robert mentioned a few weeks ago...some place to rent...what was it? Then it came to her. "I know of a house on Olivia Street. I've always thought it was adorable. My husband's a realtor. *Smith and Smith Realty*. He told me a few weeks ago that the woman living

111

there is looking for a roommate to share expenses. I don't know if it's rented or not. Shall I check?"

Katherine nodded. "That would be great." She didn't seem excited by the offer.

Chapter 30   Cici
December, then

Bryan decided to have a party to celebrate his fifth year anniversary at the restaurant. The Sunrise Café was closed for the day. He invited Cici along with André and Napoléon, Bryan's aunt and uncle, and other relatives as well as the Sunrise employees. The party was pot-luck, and everyone brought family specialties. Napoléon brought deliciously spicy Haitian rice and beans. André brought a variety of breads and Cici brought a tray of chocolate éclairs and lemon tarts. There were Cajun, Mexican, Cuban and down-home American dishes. In the morning they set up a long table in the restaurant, big enough for over thirty people. At three o'clock Bryan began heating the grill for the marinated chicken and flank steak.

Cici was introduced as a friend who was also in the food business. She liked Bryan's aunt and uncle, who encouraged her to call them Sally and Michael. Sally was a pretty blond. Cici thought she must be ADD because she couldn't sit still for a minute. She was always bustling. Her gaze was direct and no-nonsense, her laughter full and robust. Her skin bore the ravages of living in a sun-filled climate and reminded Cici to be vigilant about wearing a hat and sunscreen if she didn't want to wrinkle up like a prune.

Michael was laid back, moved slowly and spoke deliberately. His face was kind and his eyes held a sparkle. He was half again as tall as his wife and probably weighed twice as much. Cici wondered how he had managed the restaurant considering his methodical manner. She thought of cooks and waiters as always in a hurry, racing against the clock. But

113

maybe an unhurried, purposeful pace could get the job done equally well.

Michael manned the bar and made mojitos and margaritas. There was beer and wine, and pop for the kids. Everyone helped themselves from a buffet set up on one side of the room.

At the long table in the back, Cici was seated between an eight year-old boy named Carson and his father, Chet, who turned out to be Bryan's cousin. Chet looked older than Bryan. He ran a charter fishing fleet and was busy year round with vacationing fishermen. He was also a local historian. Chet told Cici about Henry Flagler, the philanthropist who had started the Standard Oil Company with the Rockefellers and was responsible for much of Florida's growth. "Henry built the Florida Overseas railroad that ran all the way to Key West," Chet said. "Everybody thought he was crazy, but it ran until a hurricane destroyed it in 1935." Chet clearly loved Key West. Cici had lots of questions and they didn't stop talking all the way through dinner.

Carson listened as well and chimed in periodically. He had obviously learned a lot from his Dad. Both of them told Cici about the Little Conch baseball league. Carson was a first baseman and had hit a home run the night before.

Later, Cici asked Chet if his wife was in the crowd.

"No, it's just us. Right, buddy?" Chet ruffled Carson's hair.

"Uh-huh." Carson was concentrating on his chocolate éclair.

"My wife is gone." He studied Carson, who continued to eat.

"Is this hard to make?" Carson asked, licking the chocolate ganache off his spoon.

"No, not at all. If you want and your dad says it's okay, you can come by the bakery and I'll teach you how."

"That would be cool. I know how to make chocolate chip cookies and Jell-O already." He turned to his father. "Can I have another one, Dad?"

"Sure thing, kiddo."

Nothing more was said about Chet's wife. Had she died or had she left him?

Later when the party was over, Cici and Bryan took a walk down to the Sunset Pier with Brandy trotting along beside them.

"Did you have a good time?" Bryan asked.

"Yes, I did. Everyone was very friendly. I liked your cousin and his little boy. I learned a lot about Key West and Florida."

"Chet could talk your ear off. He's always loved history. He went to the University of Florida and got fantastic grades but he came back here and developed his fishing fleet. I've never understood why he didn't end up in academia. I think it had to do with his wife."

"What happened to her?"

"She left Chet and went up to the mainland about five years ago. I bet Carson doesn't really remember her."

Chapter 31   Leah
Now

Kate had just left the office. Her demeanor had been secretive and superficial. They hadn't advanced in her therapy session. Leah had wanted to rehash Kate's relationship with Sam but there had been nothing new. When Leah had probed, Kate had been evasive. It was as though she were just going through the motions.

Leah was thinking about the last few weeks. Although Kate had faced some of her demons, she still maintained a dark core that refused to be revealed.   Leah didn't know if her own conclusions were due to an overactive imagination or an enlightened intuition. But she felt sure Kate was hiding something.

Leah walked over to her desk and placed her notebook square on the blotter. She hadn't written down much during today's session. She walked over to the window and opened the blinds. Outside in the morning light people walked by with purpose in their step. They were going to work or maybe the beach. The day was fresh and new. But what about Kate's day?

The thing about grief, depression and guilt, Leah mused, was that they left no visible signs to the human eye. When someone had a broken leg, a suppurating lesion or a bleeding wound, society responded with empathy. But when someone was suffering internally, bleeding emotionally, the wounds were invisible to society. Leah felt that a figurative dagger to the heart could be more debilitating than the real thing.

Chapter 32   Kate

February, now

Tomorrow was the one-year anniversary. From her tiny studio apartment, the one she would soon vacate, Kate called Cyril to tell him she wouldn't be able to go for brunch at the Morrisons. "I just feel yucky, Cyril. You guys will have to go without me."

"Are you sure? They love hearing your ideas. Particularly Barb Morrison…"

She could hear the disappointment in his voice. "I'm truly sorry, but I'm going to lay low. Please apologize for me."

"Well, okay. Take care of yourself." His voice had turned gruff.

"Cyril, goodbye and thanks for everything.

"What? Goodbye? Right. Okay." He hung up.

That call had added one more lie to a tower of lies. What difference would one more untruth, one more falsehood, one more fib make? Neil and Cyril undoubtedly saw her as a troubled soul, but they had no idea what she had done and who she really was. They had accepted that she wore black in honor of her deceased mother, not as a symbol of the murder of a child. But nothing mattered now. She wouldn't be seeing them again.

She lay on the bed in the dark waiting for midnight. Her mind was churning. Had she put everything in order? Her mind clicked through all her preparations. At 12:01 she switched on the light. One year ago the storm had raged in Lakeland. One year ago Betsy had died. One year ago Kate's life had changed forever. She stood up quickly and felt dizzy. Clutching the back of a chair, she waited for the feeling to pass. Under the sink, a two-liter bottle of red wine waited for her.

117

She'd been planning this for months. There had been a few hopeful days lately, but then the darkness came back, and she knew there was no point resisting.

She switched on the light over the kitchen sink and found the corkscrew. When the bottle was open, she took a swig from it. The warm wine slid down her throat and burned her stomach as she poured eight ounces into a chipped coffee mug. On the counter was a dark plastic bottle of Zoloft pills that she'd been saving. She opened the plastic cap and shook out the blue pills. Would she take them now? No, she would wait.

After pulling on some sweatpants and a sweatshirt, she opened the door and stepped out onto the small landing that served as her patio. There was just enough room for one stained plastic lawn chair. She carried her mug out and placed it on the wooden railing. The air was chilly, so she went back inside and brought out the bottle of wine and a blanket. She wrapped herself in the blanket and curled up in the lawn chair. The moment was near.

The wine warmed her and smoothed out the sharp edges. The anguish she felt these days was low-level compared to a year ago. Then, the heartache had been unbearable. She compared it to having a leg amputated with no anesthesia. She imagined the open nerve endings, the severed bone, the slashed muscles. Nothing could be more painful, right? But that wasn't true. She had endured psychological pain ten times more severe. Raw guilt and sharp loss had severed her heart.

At this hour, Key West was throbbing. February brought the tourists and they were out on the town; drinking, eating, laughing. This was the week of their dreams…the week they had anticipated during the long, dreary, snow-filled days of January. Was Key West the panacea for all their problems? Were they experiencing a weekend of total happiness?

118

Kate took a long drink.

It was curious to be living in a destination town. There was a disconnect between the snowbirds and the worker ants who lived here all year. The worker ants, along with the sunshine and the heat, supplied that happiness quotient for the tourists.

At one point she thought she might be one of them. Dr. Leah had given her the name of a woman with a cute house on Olivia, but she'd never called. In her heart of hearts, she knew she would no longer be here. Not after this anniversary.

She filled up her coffee mug again and took another long drink. The wine went down more smoothly now. Her body had become reacquainted with its old friend.

Maybe she could do it now. In the closet on a shelf was a length of rope she had bought months ago. She would tie one end of the rope to the banister where her wine was now sitting. For months now, she had been anticipating this day. For her to die and join Betsy on this anniversary seemed perfect.

But her mind felt muddled. Now there was Cyril and Neil…and Dr. Leah. They all seemed to care about her. Or did they? For the last few weeks she had gone back and forth. Sometimes she wanted it over and then she would feel she could go on.

No. Ultimately, she was alone. You entered this world alone and you exited the same way. She unwrapped the blanket from around her legs and tried to stand but she tripped on the bundle at her feet and fell over, hitting her head on the doorjamb. She got up on all fours and grabbed the door handle to pull herself up. She could feel warm blood running down her forehead. She had to get inside and get that rope before she changed her mind; before she was too drunk to wrap it around her neck and jump.

Chapter 33   Leah

February, now

Leah and Robert had gone to a play at the Waterfront
Playhouse. It was a comedy that had kept them laughing.
Sometimes Robert fell asleep when she dragged him to a play
in the evening but tonight he had really enjoyed it. Afterwards
they went for a drink at the Blue Parrot Bar and held hands
under the counter as they sat hip to hip on the tall stools.
Robert pushed a lock of hair from her cheek and leaned over to
kiss her. She turned her face to his and kissed him lightly on
the lips.

    He looked into her eyes. "Love you, babe."

    "The feeling is mutual." Her lips brushed his again.
They were lucky to have a relationship that kept on growing.
At the end of the day, he was the *numero uno* in her life. "I
feel extraordinarily happy I met you," Leah breathed in his ear.

    "Incredibly?"

    "Amazingly!"

    "Exceptionally?"

    "Astonishingly!"

    They laughed and kissed again. He leered at her. "Hey,
let's go home. I want to rip off your clothes and ravish you."

    She giggled. "Sounds like a plan."

    They both stood up. He put a twenty on the bar and
pulled her towards the door. Outside it was cool. Leah
wrapped her sweater around her shoulders, shivering.

    "I'll go get the car. Be back in a jiff." Robert went
down the street. As Leah stepped back inside the bar, her cell
phone vibrated in her purse. She pulled it out and looked at the
screen. It was the answering service.

Not now, she thought, but answered anyway. "Hello, Dr. Zuckerman speaking."

Chapter 34   Kate
February, now

Kate had attached the rope to the railing. She made a tight knot that wouldn't give. She was almost ready. She just needed to make the noose at the other end. Then she would jump over the railing and it would be over. She must not give in to fear. She sat down on the top step, holding the mug in her two hands.

It was too bad about the new job. Harry Stein had been happy with the latest designs she'd sent him. But was that a reason to live? The drawings meant money. But accumulating money meant nothing to her.   Next summer when the probate judgment was finalized, she would have been reasonably well off. After tonight that money from her inheritance would go to Timmy when he was twenty-one. She had set it up that way.

Kate felt bad about Dr. Leah. She would probably feel she had failed with Kate. Sometimes after a session, Kate had felt released, ready to go on with life. But deep down inside, she had kept this escape in mind.

She got up and stumbled into the studio to find the tattered picture Timmy had drawn. It was in the desk drawer. On top of the picture was the latest letter from Sam. She hadn't opened it. Why not do it now? Feel that anger pour over her. Trembling, she ripped open the envelope and pulled out the single piece of paper inside.

Kat –
Having trouble with Tim. The shrink says he needs his mother. I'm thinking about sending him down to you. Daniella and I are getting fed up with his antics. She can take just so much. You screwed him up big time. We're using tough love but I don't have the patience. I'll be in touch.

It was unsigned. Her heart did a flip-flop. Would she actually get Timmy? Was there hope? Legally, she had given up all rights to her son. She groped for the desk chair and sat down, her heart fluttering in her chest.

Chapter 35 Leah

February, now

When Robert drove up to the curb, Leah hopped in.

"Something's come up. After we get home, I'm going on a house call."

"At this hour? You're nuts. You don't do house calls."

"This is a special case. I don't know what the ethics board would think but I'm going over there."

"I want you in bed with me. Remember…five minutes ago?" He was frowning.

"I know darling but this is an emergency. I'll come wake you up when I get home and fulfill your every fantasy."

He sighed, shaking his head. "Do what you need to do. I'll wait up for you."

When Leah pulled up in front of the old Victorian house, she saw lights blazing on the top floor. She got out of the car, locked it and walked to the path that led around to the side of the house. It was dark and she tripped over a scooter that someone had left in the walkway.

In back she looked up at the wooden staircase that led up to Katherine's apartment. It didn't look too secure. She held on to the banister as she trudged up the three flights to the top floor. As she came around the last set of stairs, she looked up. Katherine was leaning on the railing, looking down at her. Her face was radiant. She began speaking before Leah reached the landing.

"It's the anniversary of my daughter's death, Black Friday. I was going to kill myself tonight." Her voice was slurred, as if she'd been drinking. "But I'm not going to now."

As Leah stepped onto the landing outside Katherine's studio, she looked down at the rope that was curled like a snake on the wooden planks at Katherine's feet. At one end was a noose. The other end was knotted to the railing. She looked at Katherine, who held a big bottle of wine in one hand. Dried blood marred her forehead and there were reddish stains— blood and red wine—on her sweatshirt.

Concealing her shock, Leah slid a hand under Katherine's elbow. "Let's go inside and you can tell me what's going on."

Chapter 36   Cici

February, now

It was the one-year anniversary. Cici had been dreading the date for weeks. She told André she wouldn't be in to work the next day. It was a Sunday and they were usually pretty busy until closing time at two. "I'm sorry, André," she'd told him, just before closing time. I just can't work tomorrow. I'll be going nuts." Her eyes were wide with apprehension.

"Don't you think maybe it would be better to work; not to dwell on that day?"

She fumbled for words. "I want to take the day…to remember…to honor the memory…of that little girl. I owe her that…"

"*Mais, mon amie*, don't you do that already…every day?" Out of respect, he didn't look at her.

"Maybe…but this is a very important anniversary for me. It changed my life. André, I can't work…please understand?"

"*D'accord*, we will manage without you." He patted her arm with his big paw.

This morning, Cici woke up before daylight. A cool breeze came in through the open window and she got up to shut it. She wanted to go to the six AM mass at the Catholic Church. As a child she'd gone to mass every Sunday with her mother. At sixteen, she'd rebelled and refused to go. Nevertheless she'd always felt a little guilty when she saw her mother scurrying around getting ready.

Cici took a shower, then dressed in long black pants and dug a warm sweater out of a box to wear over a short-sleeved blouse. It rarely was this chilly in Key West. The temperatures had been in the high seventies most of the month, but today it was fifty degrees. She let Brandy out, made herself a cup of café au lait and toasted a thick slice of bread. She spread strawberry jam on top. Then she sat at the counter sipping the hot coffee. She only took a few bites of toast. Her stomach was in knots. It was time to get going.

Outside the street was dark and there was very little traffic. It was an eight-block hike to the basilica of Saint Mary Star of the Sea. Cici had wandered the grounds of the church last fall when she was getting acquainted with Key West. This was the first time she had actually stepped inside the basilica. She slid into a wooden pew at the back of the church. She felt like a party crasher, never having attended mass there before. She had denied religion for ten years, and yet now in a time of need, she turned to the Church. It seemed like the right place to be to remember Betsy. What did that say about her rejection of the Church and her faith?

The crowd was not large and no one was paying any attention to her. She looked around the nave. The interior was pristine with clean white walls and light blue trim. Cici found herself drawn into the familiarity of the service even though it had been years. The rhythm of the liturgy was a balm to her spirit. The music poured over her. She had been so very afraid of this day, but it felt right to be here.

When the mass was over she remained in her seat. She had nowhere else she wanted to be. People poured in for the seven-thirty mass, the nine and the ten-thirty. She stayed through them all and prayed for Betsy and her family. How were they? Should she reach out to the mother and father? Would they welcome her honest apology or would it tear open a newly closed wound?

She let her mind wander and thought about the past year. So much had happened. The accident had brought her great pain, but also healthy, radical changes. Her life had taken

127

a new trajectory. Now she felt more alive. She owed her recovery to the people around her. There had been an outpouring of love from Maman, Oscar, André, Napoléon. They had all given her the time she needed to wade through the river of sorrow.

At noon, she left the basilica and realized she was starving. She stopped at Garbo's Grill for a couple of fish tacos and took them down to the dock by the water. They tasted delicious. Sitting there in the sun, she felt invisible. A constant parade of tourists strolled by. Their voices ramped up, exhilarated. But she felt pleasantly alone. It struck her that you could feel more alone in a crowd than by yourself.

Eventually, Cici meandered home. After feeding and walking Brandy, she fell into bed and slept for three hours.

When she woke up, she went downstairs, poured a glass of lemonade and sat down at her desk. She sharpened a pencil and pulled out a new notebook from the shelf. It was purple. She began to write down the thoughts that had crowded her brain that morning: *This is the anniversary of the death of Elisabeth Tripp.*

PART 3—TRICKING FATE

"Accept the things to which fate binds you, and love the people with whom fate brings you together, but do so with all your heart."

—Marcus Aurelius, *Meditations*

February-April

Chapter 36 Cici

Cici came home a little early. She tidied up the living room, put away magazines and books. In the kitchen, she filled the dishwasher and wiped down the counters. Outside she swept up the deck and watered the pots of geraniums. Everything looked neat and tidy.

Hopefully, this woman would work out. She had already interviewed a bunch of candidates. One middle-aged lady was nice but couldn't stop talking. Cici didn't think she could stand living with her. The weird girl with spiky hair definitely smelled of marijuana and tobacco, even though she claimed she didn't smoke. One woman was afraid of dogs even though Brandy was a total sweetheart. A gay guy showed up, but he said he wanted to bring friends up to his room. Cici didn't have anything against gays, but this guy seemed like a swinger and he made her uneasy.

She looked at the clock. The woman should be showing up about now. Just then the doorbell rang. She told Brandy to sit and went to the door. On the porch stood a tall woman, maybe five-nine and super-thin, dressed in black with dyed black hair. Giving her a once-over, Cici saw the woman was clean and neat. Her face was arresting, with almond-shaped green eyes and white, white skin. She carried a large-brimmed black straw hat and wore black leather sandals.

The woman was checking her out too. Cici had changed into a light blue shirt and white shorts. Her feet were bare, so this woman towered over her.

Cici smiled and said, "Please come in. I'm Cécile Lebon, better known as Cici."

"Hi, I'm Katherine Gifford, better known as Kate." The woman's smile was genuine but she seemed a little nervous. Then she saw Brandy and her face lit up. "Oh, you have a dog. I love dogs." She bent down and Brandy came over, wagging her tail. Brandy knew a dog-lover when she saw one.

"That's Brandy; she's kind of a rescue dog. She just showed up at my door with a note on her collar. Her master abandoned her."

"That's terrible, I guess…but lucky for you." She scratched Brandy's ears, then stood.

"How about a tour of the house first and then we can talk," Cici said.

"Sure, that would be great."

Kate seemed to love the place. She made comments about each room. She liked the pink and green accents in the living room and the cheery yellow and white kitchen. Out on the patio, she sat down for minute on a chaise and looked around. "This is like a secret garden." She bent over and trailed her fingers in the pool. "It's a magic place."

"Did you like that book when you were a kid? *The Secret Garden*? I did." Cici asked.

"By Frances Hodgson Burnett? Me too." Kate nodded in agreement.

They went back inside, and Cici pointed out the library nook. "I'll clear some space on the shelves if you want to store some books. We could even put in another chair and you can use the right-hand side of the counter."

Kate looked into the alcove. "Are you a writer?"

"Well, not really. But I usually write in a journal every night." She pointed out the spiral notebooks on the shelf.

"I don't keep a diary, but they say it's a healthy thing to do." Kate turned to her. "I'm trying to be a graphic artist."

Cici raised her eyebrows. "Trying to be…?"

"Well, I haven't had formal training, but there's this company that wants to buy some of my designs. So I work on them at night."

"That's cool."

Cici led the way upstairs. "My room is here on the left, and this is the room you would have." She ushered Kate into the newly decorated room.

"Oh, this is so pretty." Kate stepped into the sunny bedroom, admiring the flowered comforter and crisp curtains. She looked into the closet and pulled out a dresser drawer. "I love the colors."

For someone who loved color, Cici wondered why she dressed all in black. Maybe it was a uniform.

After Kate had checked out the bathroom, they went into the small hallway. Cici pointed to the other door. "That's a storeroom. It's unfinished but there's plenty of room to store suitcases or boxes."

Kate nodded. "Sounds great."

"Let's go downstairs and talk. Would you like a glass of lemonade?" Cici asked.

"That would be very nice. Thank you."

Cici went into the kitchen. She filled two glasses with ice, poured in the lemonade and added a sprig of mint.

Her guest was sitting on the sofa with a straight back and neatly folded hands and ankles. *She must have gone to a girl's finishing school*, Cici thought. "Here. I hope it's sweet enough. I pick the lemons right off the tree out there and squeeze them myself." She handed Kate a glass and a napkin.

Kate took a sip. "Yum. That's good. Just right. Thank you."

Cici sat down on the armchair, pushing the striped pillow off to the side. "Tell me a little about yourself. Are you from around here? Do you have a job?"

Kate sat up straighter. "I've only been here since last August. I come from a small town in Indiana. Up until now, I've been living in a furnished studio apartment. It's all right... but they've sold the building, so I have to move out."

"That's a bummer."

"Yeah. So that's why I'm here." She smiled briefly at Cici, then looked down into her glass of lemonade. "I work at *C & N Interiors*, you know, that shop on Simonton. I run the front of the store. I've been there six months. You can give them a call and check up on me." She took a card from her purse and handed it to Cici.

"I know where that is. I've walked by there. The windows always catch my eye."

Kate smiled. "Doing the windows is part of my job."

"I work at Guérin's Bakery. It's not far away," Cici said.

"Over near Virginia Street?"

Cici nodded.

"Everything in those windows looks delicious. But I've never been inside." Kate reached over and placed her unfinished lemonade on the glass-topped table.

There was a moment of silence. "Tell me why you moved down to Florida," Cici said.

More silence. Then Kate spoke. "My mother died last summer. She had Alzheimer's and I had no one else. So I decided to make a move and try something new." She avoided Cici's eyes. "I'm still wearing black to honor her."

"You must feel very alone in the world."

"I do. That's why I decided I should find a roommate." She looked up at Cici, her pale cheeks reddening.

"I feel a little that way too." Cici found herself blushing as well. She cleared her throat. "Well, I'm from Chicago and the guy who runs the bakery is a friend of the family. His wife died a year ago and he needed help so I

133

moved down. Like you, I wanted to try something new. And get away from winter…from the snow… and the cold." She shivered involuntarily.

"I know exactly how you feel. Winter is brutal in the Midwest." Kate paused and swallowed. "It's the season of reckoning…" Her voice trailed off. She was fingering the silver locket that hung around her neck.

Cici wondered what she meant by that, but the statement resonated. *The season of reckoning…*She shook herself. "Do you have a car? Parking can be a problem around here. But I have a carport you could use."

"No, I don't have a car. I don't really need one here."

"I don't either. I walk or take the bus."

"Is there anything else you want to know about me?" Kate was twisting her fingers.

"No, I don't think so." Cici paused. "Are you interested in the room?"

"Oh yes, I love it. I would keep it clean and I could help around the house if you want me to? Or I could take care of the garden. I'd do anything." Her voice was eager and her face was warm with color.

"I think we might be a good fit." Cici smiled. "Let me talk to the realtor and I'll get back to you. Is that all right?"

"Sure, great! I'll be waiting for your call." Kate stood up abruptly. She went over to Brandy and crouched down to give her a pat. The dog gazed at her lovingly. That was when Cici decided Kate would be her new roommate.

Chapter 37   Cici

Kate was moving in today after work. Cici had arranged a
bouquet of flowers in a royal blue vase and put them on the
dresser up in Kate's room.   She felt happy and anxious at the
same time. She'd been living alone for three years, except for
the months at home after the accident. It would be a big
change, sharing her home with a stranger.

Two days ago she'd talked to Robert Smith. "We did
the background check on Katherine Gifford," he'd said. "She
seems A-okay. She's from a small town in Indiana, seems to
have grown up there, gone to college and lived there most of
her life. Let's see…" She heard paper rustling. He must be
reading from a printout.

"Anything else?" Cici asked. She had Robert on
speaker-phone and was brushing Brandy.

"Well, she was married for about six years and moved
to a town outside of Chicago. Let's see…where did I see
that…Oh, Cécile, can you hold on? I've got another call. I'll
tell them I'll call back…" He was gone.

Brandy rolled over on her back. She wanted a tummy
rub. Cici gave her one, and then Robert came back on the line.
"Hi, I'm back. So where was I?" He sounded rushed.

"You were saying Katherine Gifford was married."

"Oh right, she was married and divorced…Hmm…
Her credit is good although she doesn't have a long credit
history. It dates back to last summer. She's been at *C & N
Interiors* since September."

"I called Cyril Johnson and he vouched for her." Cici
said. As a matter of fact, he's wild about her. I got the feeling
he was glad she might be moving in with me."

"Those guys at C & N are really great. I would trust their endorsement."

"Good! I'm going to give her a call. Thank you for your help, Robert."

Cici heard the doorbell ring and hurried to the door. Kate stood there sandwiched between two gentlemen. That was definitely the term. They looked to be fifty or sixty and stood protectively on each side of Kate. Beyond them in the street, she saw a white van.

Cici held out her hand. "Welcome."

Kate was smiling. "Let me introduce Cyril Johnson and Neil Hughes. They've kindly agreed to help me move in.

Cyril had an oval-shaped bald head and bright blue eyes. He wore a yellow and blue-dotted bow tie, a blue vest and a sparkling white shirt. His smile was broad and sincere. "It is jolly to meet you. What a gem of a house."

"Lovely to meet you. Please call me Neil." The other man wore a dove-grey suit with a pink and white striped shirt. He had wavy grey hair and crinkly deep-set grey eyes. A warm smile lit his face.

Neither man was dressed for moving heavy boxes. But as it turned out, there wasn't much to do. Neil, who walked with a cane, came in to sit in the living room while Cici and Cyril helped Kate carry in two suitcases, two boxes, four grocery bags of miscellaneous items, and a laptop. That was it.

"That's all? " Cici asked.

"I moved down here with just two suitcases. My last place was furnished. I haven't bought much since I arrived."

Once everything was placed in the bedroom, they went down to the living room. "May we look around?" Cyril asked.

Cici nodded. "Sure, but there's not much to see."

"Cyril, check out the library alcove," Neil said. "What a great use of space."

Cyril was eyeing the glass-topped table. "Where did you find this? It's got a lot of pizzazz."

Neil stepped out on to the patio. "Love the garden and pool. It must be a great spot to unwind at the end of the day."

Cici was busy thinking while they looked around. Bryan had offered to supply dinner tonight and meet her new roommate. She had agreed because she was nervous and wanted to use him as a buffer this first night. Now she thought they could make a party of it. "How would you like to stay for supper? A friend of mine who's a chef is bringing dinner over."

Cyril looked at Neil. "Are you sure? We don't want to put you out."

"I think it would be fun…a celebration. Let me call Bryan and see what he's planning."

Bryan said there would be enough food for everyone. He arrived a half hour later with a pan of seafood lasagna and a spinach, walnut and strawberry salad. Kate helped Cici set the table. There was a baguette from the bakery and Cyril opened a bottle of Riesling. They settled down to a gala dinner.

Cyril was a natural comedian and Neil played his sidekick. Cici felt glad they were there. It helped to ease Kate and herself into their new relationship. Bryan was a real addition, sharing stories about Key West. Neil and Cyril had eaten many times in the Sunrise Café and knew Bryan by sight.

"Bryan, this lasagna is delicious. What's in it?" Kate asked.

"Let's see. There's shrimp, scallops, lobster, wine, cream, parmesan, and fresh noodles." In the lamplight, Bryan's blond hair shone. Cici admired the smooth planes of his face, his strong chin and intelligent eyes. Of course, they were just friends but tonight she looked at him in a new light.

"You're quite the chef," Neil said.

"Well, thank you. I hope to improve and develop some new techniques. In May, I'm leaving for a month, going to New York. I'll be working under a world-renowned chef in a three-star restaurant. It'll be a great opportunity to polish my skills."

Neil chuckled. "I suppose toiling away in another chef's kitchen is an opportunity but it sounds exhausting to me."

When they had finished, Kate cleared the table while Cici scooped lemon sorbet into small glass bowls and poured a few spoonfuls of crème de menthe over the top. It had been her mother's go-to summer dessert.

"Delicious, my dear," Cyril said. He smiled at her and then looked around the room. "You know, we could spice up this room if you'd like. Just a few changes… and I've got a couple of things at the shop that would look nice in here."

Taken aback, Cici said, "Well, I don't know. I guess so."

"Don't let Cyril push you around," Neil said. "He's always full of ideas."

Cyril was already up and moving towards the sofa. "If you don't like it, we'll switch it back. How does that sound?"

She, Kate and Neil watched, bemused, as Cyril enlisted Bryan's help and moved the furniture around. After that, they drove over to *C & N Interiors* and came back with a silver-framed mirror, three framed prints, an elegant console table, a ceramic pot in a swirl of colors and a small lamp with a Tiffany glass shade. They hung the mirror in the entryway over the console table, placed the pot to the left on the table and the lamp on the right. In the main room Cyril centered the prints over the sofa; and then Bryan came back from the van with a box. Inside was an exquisite multi-colored carved giraffe that Cyril placed in a corner near the door to the patio. Along with it came three ceramic gold finches that Cyril set on an empty

138

shelf in the kitchen. The little birds looked like they were having a conversation.

Cyril was in his zone, oblivious of everyone. When he'd finished, he turned to her. "Voilà, Mademoiselle, is this to your liking?"

Cici went to check out the entryway and then circled the living area. The room had come together. "I don't know what to say. It looks fabulous, but Cyril, I can't pay you for all these lovely objects."

"Don't worry about that. This is stuff I've had in the warehouse for years. If I ever really need anything I'll come back and borrow it. Okay?" He was beaming.

"Don't worry your pretty little head," Neil said. "Cyril does this all the time. He might get an idea tonight and come back tomorrow with an Egyptian mummy. You never know."

Cici stepped over and gave Cyril a big hug. "Thank you so much. You are a genius."

He grinned wider. "All in a day's work, my dear."

Chapter 38   Kate

Kate woke up late. It was almost eight o'clock. She hadn't slept this well for months. It was probably due to the lovely meal and good companionship. She was glad Cyril and Neil had stayed for dinner. It had been a fun evening. She hadn't done anything social since Black Friday.

Bryan seemed like a really nice guy. She couldn't figure out if he was just a friend of Cici's or something more. After Cyril and Neil had left, Cici and Bryan went out on the front porch. From upstairs Kate had heard them talking quietly...probably about her. Then he'd left.

She grabbed her cotton bathrobe and padded downstairs. There was a thermos of coffee on the counter with a note. *Good morning. I hope you slept well. There are eggs, sliced bread, jam, OJ. Please help yourself. I'll be home at 3:30-4ish. Cici P.S. I like your friends a lot!!!* Of course Cici was already gone. She went to work at six.

Kate poured some coffee and took it out to the patio. She sat down on a chaise and smiled to herself. Her every sense was turned on high. She smelled the sweetly perfumed flowers, tasted the rich coffee and heard the chirping birds. She savored them all and felt happy. Yes, happy for the first time since forever... partly because of her new residence, but mainly because of Timmy. One day she would hold him in her arms again, kiss the top of his head and smell his little-boy smell. She had read Sam's note over and over. Ultimately, he would have no patience for Timmy. But she worried about what Sam meant when he said they were using "tough love." What did that mean? Was it physical or mental or both?

Her happy mood had given way to the familiar angst. She got up and began to pace the wooden deck around the pool. She was perspiring and her head was pounding. *God, get a grip.* She said to herself.

She looked at the pool. The cool water beckoned. She ripped off her bathrobe, tee-shirt and panties. Then she plunged nude into the water. It was cold at first. She stayed under until her body screamed for air. When she resurfaced she took deep breaths, feeling cleansed and purified. Slowly, she swam back and forth the length of the small pool.

She had to take control of her life. She had a choice every day to wallow in pain or accept her fate and move on. Feeling sorry for herself, feeling guilty, wouldn't get her anywhere. She needed to choose life, choose a future…and be ready for Timmy.

The thought blossomed in her head, a major revelation. It felt like being knocked off a horse…or being reborn. Feeling light headed and strangely calm, Kate got out of the pool and wrapped herself in her bathrobe. She was hungry, starving in fact.

She made scrambled eggs and toast, then after breakfast went upstairs and put away her few possessions. She opened the attic door off the hallway to stow her suitcase and empty boxes. The attic had a slanted roof and two dormer windows covered with dark shades. It was big enough to be turned into a third bedroom.

Kate took a shower and got dressed. In the mirror, she eyed the quarter-inch of red roots that had grown out in the past three weeks. What would Timmy think of her black hair? He wouldn't even recognize her. It was time to become herself again. She would let her hair grow out, maybe even cut it short like Cici's?

Downstairs, Kate went into the office alcove to get her laptop. She wanted to take it to the shop today so she could work on her latest project if there was down time. The new design was a spring flower theme with greens, yellows and blues. On the counter that served as a desk, a spiral notebook lay open. As she reached for her laptop, she glanced at the open page. Cici had a neat, precise hand. The first line read: *My new roommate moved in last night. I like her a lot. I think we'll get along well. She seems kind and sensitive, but I sense a darkness within her.*

Kate stopped reading. Darkness within her…that was an apt evaluation. She needed to be careful around Cici. Her roommate had keen antennae.

Chapter 39   Cici

Things had slowed down at the bakery. Cici checked on the ovens. Fifteen minutes before the babas needed to come out. She had already prepared the rum syrup to bathe the cakes while they were still warm. She sat down outside at one of the little round tables next to Brandy and absentmindedly caressed the dog's ears as she sipped on a Diet Coke. This afternoon she needed a little caffeine to give her a jump start.

She'd enjoyed last night. It had been fun. Kate's buddies were an entertaining couple. At first she'd been leery when Cyril suggested redecorating her house, but he'd created wonders in a short period of time.

Kate was pleasant to be around. She seemed a little reserved, but that was fine with Cici. She still wondered about the dyed hair. Last night she'd noticed that Kate's natural hair color was either red or strawberry blond. It seemed weird that she would do this all-black thing for her deceased mother. They must have been especially close.

Without wanting to, her mind turned to Bryan and their talk last night. After Kate went up to bed, they'd gone out on the porch. Bryan sat in the big rocking chair and she sat on his lap. They'd spent a little time cuddling and kissing.

After a while, she said, "How come you didn't tell me about this trip to New York in May?"

"Didn't want to upset you. I knew you'd be devastated." He chuckled.

"Right." She poked him in the ribs.

"You'll miss me a little, won't you?"

"Maybe a little."

They kissed again. They'd done a lot of kissing but nothing more in the past few weeks. Cici thought this was bizarre. These days, most guys tried to get girls in bed on the second date, if not the first.

"So, Bryan..."

"Yes." He kissed her on that sensitive place just behind her ear.

"How come you haven't tried to jump my bones?"

"Jump your bones?" He cracked up. "Jump your bones? Where did that come from?"

"You know what I mean. How come you haven't dragged me into bed with you?"

He was silent for a long moment. Then he said quietly, "Because I care too much about you. I want everything to go just right."

Cici felt touched, and a little abashed. They had spent a lot of time together lately. Bryan, being a Key West native, had never visited the local tourist attractions. They'd been to the Truman Little White House and the Hemingway museum, after which she'd started reading *For Whom the Bell Tolls*. Doing that was a victory of sorts; for the last year she'd been unable to concentrate well enough to read any book.

They'd been to the butterfly museum and the aquarium, as well as sharing lots of meals and listening to music in bars. Conversation was never a problem and they could be quiet together as well.

"I want everything to go right, too." Feeling a little uncomfortable with how the conversation was going, Cici yanked gently on his pony tail. "What about this ponytail thing? Have you always had it?"

"No, that started when I was in culinary school. It seemed like the in thing to do. I might cut it off when I go to New York." He paused. "Cici, I like you a lot." He swallowed. "But I think you're hiding something from me."

She pulled away and sat up straight, her heart beating rapidly. "What do you mean?"

"I just get the feeling there's part of you that you don't want to share. Something…I don't know…painful." He pulled her back against him and kissed her cheek. She could feel the warmth of a blush.

"Of course I haven't told you everything about me. I bet you have secrets too. I bet you did stuff in high school you're not proud of…" Cici's voice wavered. She didn't want to lie but she wasn't ready to tell him her secret.

"Okay. Forget it." He turned his face towards hers.

She couldn't see his eyes in the dark but she felt his appraising gaze. Then they melded together in a long, forgiving kiss.

Chapter 40   Kate

Kate's new life had fallen into a pleasant routine. In the morning, Cici left before she was awake. It gave Kate time to be alone in the house and putter around before she left for the shop. Cici came home an hour or so earlier in the afternoon and was usually sitting in the library alcove writing in her spiral notebook when Kate got home. Brandy always came bounding to greet her and Cici sang out a hello.

Since both of them worked in retail and spent the day dealing with people, they both liked some quiet time after the workday ended. Kate usually changed into her bathing suit and took a dip in the pool before dinner. Then they would fix something easy and chat as they ate. Usually dinner was a big salad with grilled fish or chicken. Sometimes Cici brought home a couple of fruit tarts for Kate because she knew Kate loved them.

Later, in the twilight, they would lay outside on the chaise lounges and drink a glass of wine. Their conversation was comfortable, though Kate sensed there were areas in Cici's life she didn't want to share. Kate understood that all too well. Cici talked about growing up in a bakery with all the laughter and bustle. Kate's rigidly controlled childhood in Indiana had been far different. Thanks to her therapy sessions, she felt able to share that part of her life.

"Kate?" Cici said one evening as they lounged on the deck.

"Huh?"

"See those sparkling stars up there? They're whispering to us."

Kate smiled. She liked Cici's quirky, poetic streak. "Yeah, it's a magical night."

146

"Did you ever read *The Little Prince*?"

"No. Why?"

"You should. It provides a map to understanding what's important in life. I've got a copy. I'll give it to you. My *maman* used to read it to me."

"Okay." Kate took a sip of wine. She allowed herself one glass in the evening now when Cici was there.

"There's this idea that when someone dies, their soul goes up to inhabit a star. So when you look at the night sky, you can imagine your loved one, up there, laughing on a star." Cici sounded tentative. "There's the same idea in the movie *The Lion King*...that ancestors look down on us from the stars."

Kate's skin flushed. She felt as if her nerves were standing on end. "It would be nice to think that someone you loved was laughing and happy..." She heard her own voice, low and tremulous, and stopped speaking.

"Kate, are you all right?"

"Yes. Just feeling a little emotional tonight." She finished her glass of wine in a single swallow.

Chapter 41   Cici

On Sunday afternoon, Cici came home at two-fifteen. Kate had spent the day working in the garden; weeding, pruning and cleaning up the front and back flowerbeds. When Cici arrived she was sitting on the front steps surveying her labors.

Cici admired the flowerbeds. "Look at all the work you've done. Everything looks so neat and tidy."

"It was fun. A lot of these plants are unfamiliar to me, so I researched online. Anyway, I feel great. It's satisfying to dig around in the dirt." She grinned at Cici, her dirt-streaked face red from the heat.

"Listen, I've got an idea. You know how you told me you want to get out of your black phase and add some color to your life?"

"Yes," Kate said slowly, a questioning look in her eyes.

"I want you to come with me to meet my friend Clarissa. She owns a clothing shop and can give you some great deals."

Kate bent down to pick up her gardening gloves and trowel. "It'll be a big change for me."

"And remember, tonight we're going to have dinner at Bryan's restaurant. He wants to try his new signature dishes on us and he's invited a couple of relatives as well. You'll like them."

"That should be fun." Kate kept her gaze averted, and her tone of voice didn't match her words.

Cici did her best to sound encouraging. "Let's get you something emerald green to match your green eyes."

Twenty minutes later, Kate had showered and changed into clean black pants and a black tee-shirt. They set out towards Duval Street. Cici hoped Clarissa would do her magic and convince Kate to buy some colorful clothes.

When they arrived at the shop, Clarissa came out from behind the counter and gave Cici a hug. They'd gotten together for dinner a couple of times, but not lately.

After introductions, Clarissa led Kate to the back of the shop. She looked her up and down and made some suggestions. Then she pulled out three dresses on hangers. "Try these on. You've got a great figure...like a model."

Kate took the dresses but then stood there, looking uncertain.

"This should be very cute on you," Clarissa continued, handing her another dress.

"Thanks," Kate said, her arms full.

The sound of a parrot-squawk interrupted them, and Clarissa laughed. "Oh oh, I've got to go up front. I'll leave you to it."

Kate looked at Cici. "I don't know if I'm ready for this."

"Here's what I think. You love color. Look at your drawings. I don't think your mother, bless her soul, wants you to wear black for the rest of your life."

Kate looked flustered but she nodded. She handed Cici the dresses and pulled off the black tee-shirt. Cici watched as Kate tried on the dresses, along with some skirts, shorts and shirts. She loosened up a little as she considered various garments. She leaned towards a blue-green palette, though Cici thought she looked great in an orange and pink flowered dress. "I love that dress on you. It will look great when your red hair grows out."

Kate giggled. "You've told me you love just about everything I've tried on."

Cici didn't think she had ever heard Kate giggle before. It made her seem younger and more alive.

149

Finally, she pulled the black tee-shirt and pants back on. "Okay, I'm going to take these three dresses, these two skirts and these four tops. I can wear them over my black pants, too."

"What about those strappy sandals and the wedges? They would go with a lot of those clothes."

Kate picked up the wedge sandals, which were bright salmon pink. She eyed them, considering. "I don't want to break the bank. But I have made some money on my latest designs. Okay, I'll take the shoes too."

Together they put back the items Kate wasn't buying and then carried her purchases to the front. Clarissa gave Kate the same deal she'd given Cici, saying, "A friend of Cici's is a friend of mine."

Back out on the street, they decided to trek down to Mattheesson's for an ice cream cone. As they ambled along licking their ice cream, Cici decided to try another suggestion. "Why don't we go over to the Smooth Sailing Salon and you could get your hair styled and trimmed?"

Kate stopped and turned to look at Cici, her eyes narrowed. "You've been planning this little outing for a while, haven't you?"

"Well, you said you were ready for a change. I'm just giving you a little nudge in that direction." She couldn't help laughing. That set Kate off, and they stood there in the street cracking up. Who knew what was so funny? But it felt good to laugh.

"Okay, devious one," Kate said finally, tears streaming down her face. "Let's go shave my head."

Fifteen minutes later, Cici dropped Kate off at the salon and went home carrying half of Kate's bags of clothes.

Chapter 42 Kate

The hairdresser's name was Zanzibar. Apparently, her mother had liked the sound of the word. Zanzibar had spiky red hair, bright black eyes and was heavily made up. Her rotund figure was stuffed into a shocking-pink tank top and a purple mini-skirt.

"Holy moly, honey," she said as Kate sat down in the styling chair. "What did you do to your hair?"

"I've been in mourning."

"Mourning? It looks to me like you've been killing off your hair. It's as dry as a witch's broom."

"I've been dyeing it with some stuff from the drug store."

"I can tell. Your hair is in mourning for sure." She picked up the long black strands with disgust. "Let's cut this off."

"I want to grow it out. You can see my roots. They're red."

"Yes, a very pretty color." Zanzibar studied her in the mirror. "Here's what I'll do. I'll cut off all this." She held up the dyed lengths of hair. "Then I'll nourish what's left with a special, rich conditioner and style it in a bob. This long straight hair does nothing for you. And your roots stand out like road signs."

When she left the salon a little while later, Kate felt like a new woman. Her stylishly tousled hair fell softly around her face. Zanzibar said it would help make her roots less noticeable. A woman sitting in the chair next to her watched the transformation. As Kate left she heard the woman say she wanted to "look like that model." Talk about positive reinforcement.

At home, Cici went wild over the haircut too. "You are just beautiful! Wear one of your new dresses tonight and you'll feel like a million dollars."

They left the house at six and walked the few blocks to the Sunrise Café. Kate wore a blue and green patterned wrap dress and her new sandals. Cici looked cool in a white lace top and blue pencil skirt. Everyone turned around when they entered the restaurant.

"Here are the girls," said a man standing behind the bar. He came around and introduced himself to Kate. "I'm Bryan's Uncle Michael. What can I get you two to drink?"

Cici asked for a margarita but Kate stuck with a glass of white wine. A blond woman bursting with energy came bustling over to greet them. "You must be the new roommate we've heard about. I'm Sally, Bryan's aunt." She hugged Cici. "We're not allowed back in the kitchen. Bryan is concocting some masterpiece."

"He's been talking to me about signature dishes...something he created. I guess it's a way of putting yourself on the culinary map," Cici said.

A table was set in the middle of the restaurant, complete with white tablecloth and sparkling crystal. A basket made of woven silver strands contained a bouquet of lilies. The setting proclaimed discreet elegance. Kate felt appropriately dressed for the occasion.

At another table a man was bent over a boy who was busy drawing on an art pad. They didn't look up at first. Cici waved Kate over. "Come meet Bryan's cousin and his little boy."

The man stood up and smiled. Kate stood frozen in place. She recognized his face, his smile, his eyes. How could this be happening? Where could she hide?

Chet frowned. Her face must be giving her away. "Are you all right?"

Cici looked at her, puzzled. "Kate, do you want to sit down? You're as white as a sheet."

Chet didn't seem to recognize her. What with the short, still-black hair and her loss of thirty pounds, she probably didn't look the same. She began to breathe easier. "No, no, I'm fine, probably just hungry. Sorry to give you all a scare." She smiled brightly and extended her hand to Chet. "What did you say your name was?"

He took her hand in a firm grip. "Chet Hunter. This is my son Carson. We're drawing battleships." He gestured to the sketchpad that lay open on the table.

Carson looked up with brown eyes like his father's. "I can't make it look right." He held the pencil in a tight fist.

Kate bent over and looked at the boy's drawing. "Here, maybe I can help." She sat down next to him and he handed her the pencil. She erased some lines, changed the angle and shaded in several areas. The ship began to take shape. Kate felt Chet and Carson watching her movements. It was all she could do not to start shaking.

"Wow, that's cool. It looks better...like a real ship." Carson smiled at her. "Can you show me how to do that?"

"Sure." She turned the page. "Can I draw here?"

"Uh-huh" The boy watched her sketch. Hesitantly, she explained how to create perspective and depth as she drew some simple examples. His arm brushed against hers and she felt something move deep inside. It was good to be sitting next to a small boy. She'd almost forgotten what that felt like.

"Ta da!" Bryan came out of the kitchen carrying several plates. "Ladies and gentlemen, please be seated."

What followed was an elegant three-course dinner. They began with a delicate she-crab soup. For the second course, Bryan had prepared a sautéed duck breast. Each plate was beautifully presented with a crispy triangle of polenta, a swirl of balsamic vinegar, thin slices of duck breast and a dab of blackberry confit.

They all began to eat. "Bryan, this is to die for," Sally said. "I want to pick up my plate and lick it off."

Michael agreed. "You've outdone yourself, my boy."

"Yes, it's a symphony of flavors." Cici chimed in.

Bryan beamed. "Pour yourselves another glass of wine while I get the dessert ready. It will take a few…"

"Are you sure you don't want help?" Cici asked.

"Maybe later." Bryan disappeared into the kitchen. Then he stuck his head back out. "There's always the dishes…"

Kate had placed herself at the opposite end of the table from Chet, worried that she might say something that would tip him off. As she sat there, she tried to remember what their online conversations had been about. That was over a year ago. Living with secrets was a tricky business, like picking your way through a field of land mines.

"Tell us about yourself," Sally said.

She must have read Kate's mind. "Oh, there's nothing much to say. I was raised in Indiana, small town you've never heard of…" Had she discussed her hometown and her parents with Chet? She couldn't remember. Everyone was looking at her expectantly.

She shrugged. "Normal childhood…I got tired of the Midwest weather and decided to try something new. That's why I moved down here." She felt herself blushing. She had never liked being in the limelight.

"Do you have any brothers or sisters?" Sally asked.

"No, I was an only child." She looked around the table. "There's nothing to know about me." She turned to Chet; nothing like looking into the lion's mouth. "How old is Carson?"

Chet studied her from across the table. "He's eight."

154

Carson said, "I'll be nine on the fourth of July. I'm an Independence Day baby."

"That's right," Kate murmured. Carson's birthday was the same as Timmy's. She remembered that now. Timmy had thought it was fun that there were fireworks in Lakeland on his birthday. Had she and Chet ever discussed that?

Chet frowned. "What's that?"

Kate had started to sweat. "The fourth of July must be a special birthday."

Thankfully, Bryan arrived then with the dessert. He had woven strands of caramel to form upside-down baskets. Inside were raspberries on a nest of meringue and whipped cream. A loop of raspberry coulis decorated each plate. Everyone applauded.

After Bryan had served his guests, he sat down next to Cici. "Here's what I wanted to tell you tonight." He looked around the table. "I've put in an offer for the house next door. The first floor has several small rooms with a nice patio in back. I'm going to join the two buildings together through the kitchens and open a second restaurant right there—an upscale bistro for dinner only."

Michael looked intrigued. "How are you going to manage that? You're busy with The Sunrise Café from morning until late afternoon. You can't work twenty-four hours a day."

"José is going to run the café. He's my sous-chef and I trust him completely. I'm going to phase myself out of the everyday operations of the place."

Michael sipped water. "Money?"

"I've got a backer. He's gung-ho! I know what you're thinking…restaurants come and go. But I'm convinced Key West doesn't have anything like what I'm planning. It's going to be a success."

Michael still didn't look convinced.

155

"I'm worried you're going to wear yourself out." Sally said.

Bryan shrugged. "I can handle it."

"With the food you served us tonight, I think you'll be a success," Kate said.

"I agree with Kate." Chet smiled at her and she smiled back. "Go for it."

Nodding at her, Bryan said, "That's part of the reason I'm going to New York in May. I need to work on a menu with eclectic fresh dishes...kick-ass flavors...the wow factor that brings people back again and again. With what I've been working on, I think I'm on the right track but I need an injection of new cooking vibes."

"Well said." Michael grinned. "Sally and I want the best for you, you know that?"

"Thanks, Michael." Bryan's eyes were bright with emotion. He turned to Cici, who hadn't said anything. "I might need a pastry chef in my new establishment. What do you think?"

All eyes were on Cici. Kate sensed her discomfort. "I'll help you every way I can, Bryan," Cici said. A funny little smile came over her face. "I think you'll make this dream a reality. If you really want the best, you'll make it happen."

She and Bryan were looking at each other as though no one else was in the room.

Chapter 43   Cici

Monday, Cici's day off, had started out fine. She'd opted to stay home and putz around. In the morning she took care of laundry, bills and some cleaning. She had lunch out by the pool: cheese, crackers, a bunch of grapes and a bottle of Perrier. She sat in the shade. The temperature was perfect. The wall of bright flowers seemed to vibrate in the sun. A mango hummingbird dipped his beak into the bird feeder that Kate had put up and then flitted around the garden. This quiet spot felt like heaven on earth.

In the afternoon, she spent a short time writing in her journal and then turned to the computer to work on her secret project. She was writing a book but she wasn't ready to share that fact with Kate or Bryan or the guys at the bakery. At this point she didn't know where it was going and she wasn't ready to divulge her aspirations. But whenever she had a free moment at work or when she was walking Brandy, her mind often went to her characters and plot line. The book had become an alternate reality.

By the time Kate came through the door, the afternoon had flown by and Cici had written over a thousand words. "Hey, I'm home," Kate's voice rang out.

"I'm in here."

Kate came into the alcove smiling. "Got a check today from Harry Stein. He really liked that last series. I just can't believe it."

Cici swiveled around to look at her. "That's great."

"And that's not all. He's talking about an article in *Living Etc...* It's this British magazine about decorating. Wouldn't that be fabulous?"

"Awesome. You're going to be famous."

157

Kate went over and plopped down on the sofa. "I just can't believe this is happening. Everyone always told me my drawing was a giant waste of time. My parents, my ex…I feel, I don't know…vindicated?"

Kate rarely mentioned her ex-husband. She never wanted to share that part of her past. From the little bit Cici had heard, he sounded like a total jerk. "Well, now you know they were wrong. You've got a great career ahead of you."

"What are you doing for dinner?" Kate asked. "Are you going out with Bryan?"

"No, I'm here."

"Good. Let's grill some fish," Kate said. "I'll just change into some shorts and run down to the market."

"Okay, I'll go with you and take Brandy for a little walk. We haven't gone anywhere all day."

A few minutes later they were out the door, each carrying a shopping basket. They chatted as they walked. Brandy kept ahead of them, stopping to sniff and baptize chosen lamp posts.

"I forgot to tell you, Chet invited us to go out on his boat next Sunday," Cici said.

Kate looked startled. "That's nice, but I don't really know him that well. Maybe I should stay home."

"Come on, Kate, it'll be fun. Bryan has been talking about doing this since I met him and we've never gone. We can try catching some mammoth deep sea fish."

"I don't know. I've never been on a boat in the ocean. I might get seasick."

"Well, you'll never know if you don't try. You could probably bring some Dramamine along, just in case."

"Well, okay. I guess I'll go."

She sounded like it would be an ordeal instead of a pleasure trip. Cici wondered what that was about. "We're going out about noon and we'll bring a picnic. Carson is coming along too. He likes you a lot."

Kate looked troubled, but tried to smile. "Yes, I like little kids."

At the market, they bought grouper caught that very day. Along with the fish, they decided to grill some corn and make a salad. Kate picked out a bottle of white wine. As she was about to pay, Cici disappeared and came back with a pint of Haagen-Dazs Dulce de Leche ice cream. This was their mutual favorite.

"Good choice," the Cuban check-out girl said. "It's my favorite, too." They all laughed as she put their purchases in the baskets.

Brandy was waiting patiently by the door. As they exited the market, she got up and started trotting down the sidewalk. Then suddenly, a black cat raced across the sidewalk right in front of her. She barked and charged after the cat.

"Oh shit," Cici said. She shoved her basket at Kate and started after him. "Brandy! Brandy, come here!" The cat careened down the sidewalk and then turned into the street. Brandy kept after it, barking. Loud honking and the screeching of tires filled the air. Brandy's barking abruptly ceased. Cici couldn't see her amid the cars that had stopped in both directions.

"Oh no!" She screamed as she ran into the street. "Where's my dog? Where's my dog?" She still couldn't see Brandy. "Brandy, Brandy."

A red-faced man got out of a black BMW and yelled at Cici. "Your damned dog almost caused an accident. He shouldn't be running loose." He spoke with a strong New Jersey accent and his tee-shirt didn't quite cover his hairy protruding stomach.

Kate ran between the cars and around the BMW. "Over here, Cici. She's over here."

Cici heard the vibrations of the car engines and felt the heat reflected from the pavement. Everything was too vivid, like a bad dream. Could this really be happening? She followed Kate and found Brandy lying on the pavement near the curb. The dog was breathing heavily, her tongue lolling out of her mouth. Kate was crooning to the dog as she gently patted Brandy's head. "It's all right, good girl…"

"Is she okay?" Shakily, Cici bent down and moved her hands along Brandy's chest and abdomen, then felt along her legs. "There's my good girl. You okay?"

Brandy eyed her, panting heavily. She didn't cry out or react as if in pain as Cici's hands moved over her.

Cici could feel the tears coming. "Oh, Brandy. Can you stand up? Come on, good girl!" She straightened, stepped back a little and beckoned the dog to come. The dog pushed up on her front paws and then got her hind legs under her. She stood up, shook herself and then padded over to Cici, wagging her tail.

"I think she's all right." Kate said. Then she burst into tears.

Cici turned and hugged her, crying too. "I was so afraid she'd been killed. I couldn't stand to lose her. I should have had her on a leash. Then this never would have happened."

Kate took a ragged breath. "It's not your fault. She saw that cat and took off."

"She could have been killed." Cici's voice broke.

"Cars are instruments of death." Kate murmured.

The guy from New Jersey shook his head, got back in his car and took off. Traffic started up again. Brandy sat down on the grass and watched them, her head cocked to one side.

Chapter 44   Kate

Sunday turned out to be a beautiful day. Not a cloud in the sky. Bryan picked up Cici and Kate at 9:30. The thought of spending several hours on a fishing boat with Chet filled Kate with apprehension. Could she keep her identity a secret? She would need to keep a low profile once they were on the boat.

She smiled brightly at Bryan as she helped load the car. He certainly didn't need to know how anxious she felt. She had on her bathing suit and a turquoise cover up with a matching bandana around her head. It wasn't her usual style but she didn't want Chet to notice her red roots when her hair started blowing around in the wind.

"You're going to love this boat. It's a beauty." Bryan said as he placed their cooler in the trunk.

"I am oh so ready for this day. I'm planning on just lying back and enjoying the sea breezes." Cici said.

"What a minute. You're going to be a member of the crew and haul in the fish." Bryan said as he stowed their towels.

"Right, like I know anything about fishing." Cici folded back the passenger front seat so Kate could slide into the back.

Once on the road, Kate watched Cici and Bryan's heads as they turned to smile at each other. She listened to their easy banter. They seemed so comfortable with each other. She felt a pang of jealousy. She had never had a comfortable, healthy relationship with a man.

Minutes later they arrived at the dock. Chet's fishing boat was impressive. It was two stories high and shiny white. On the stern the words *Perfect Chaos* were printed in red and black script. Since arriving in Key West, Kate had often wandered down to the marina but she had never boarded a boat. This would be a first. Cici was a neophyte as well when it came to fishing boats and nautical adventures. She had packed some Dramamine in case either of them got seasick.

Chet greeted them from above. "Welcome aboard, mates." He was wearing a red baseball cap and his face was in shadow. Kate couldn't read his expression.

A minute later, Carson's head popped up over the side. "Hi, Uncle Bryan. Hi, Cici." He shouted. His grin widened when he spied Kate. "Hi Kate."

They clambered aboard lugging the coolers, towels and beach bags. Chet met them and led the way down into the salon where they could stow their paraphernalia. Kate looked around the small room. It was neat and spotless with a mini kitchen, an oval table in a nook, and an "L" shaped sofa. Red and blue upholstery, gleaming oak cupboards with brass fittings added to the nautical charm.

"This is so cool. Everything has its place." Cici pulled out drawers and peered into cupboards.

"Yeah, every inch of this boat was carefully thought out." Kate said.

"That's the secret of a well-constructed vessel. You're dealing with limited space so every inch has to fulfill a specific need." Chet said.

Kate stepped over to the window. A yacht was tied up in the next berth. A white-haired man was reading the paper, a mug of coffee in his hand. She wondered what it would be like to live on a boat and wake up to the gentle rocking of the vessel. It seemed like an escape from everyday life. She looked up to see Chet eyeing her pensively.

Carson was hopping impatiently from one foot to the other. "Are we going to take off now Dad? You said I could help."

"Right, Carson. Come on up to the fly bridge and we'll get the motor started." Chet ruffled his son's dark curly hair.

A few minutes later, Kate could feel the vibrations of the boat's motor. She and Cici climbed out to the sundeck at the rear of the vessel and sat down on the white leather seats. Above them, Kate could see Chet and Carson talking and laughing together. Kate knew that they had a very close relationship. The boat was moving out of its berth and into the channel that led to the sea.

Bryan came from the bow where he had assisted Chet in untying the lines. He sat down next to Cici and put his arm loosely around her shoulders. They smiled at each other.

Kate put her head back and closed her eyes. She felt the sun on her face and listened to the crying of the gulls and the throbbing of the engine. Her mind wandered and when she next opened her eyes, they were through the channel and out into the ocean. She felt incredibly happy. She smiled at Cici. "You were right. I'm glad I came."

The guys spent the morning fishing while Cici relaxed in the sun. Kate and Carson played several games of War. Then they convinced Cici to play Uno with them. There was a lot of laughter. Kate and Carson ganged up on Cici and forced her hand. Then Carson's allegiance switched to Cici and they went after Kate. About 11:30 they all agreed they were starving.

Bryan had brought a variety of sandwiches, pasta salad, coleslaw and barbeque chips. Chet had beer and wine as well as soft drinks. They settled down around the table in the aft of the boat. The conversation was easy and Kate felt relaxed. They talked about the boat races coming up, traffic problems on the A1A and Bryan's plans for the new restaurant.

Kate reached in her bag and pulled out the plastic container of double chocolate chip cookies she'd made. She remembered that Chet had said he loved them. "Would you like a cookie?" She offered the container to Carson first and then his Dad. Carson took two; one in each hand.

Chet's eyes lit up. "Those look great. That's my favorite." He took two as well and passed the container to Cici.

Cici took a bite. "Yum! These are delish."

Kate smiled. "I'm honored that a famous pastry chef approves of my cookies. I was almost afraid to bake them."

Cici laughed. "But you know, there's something so comforting about chocolate chip cookies. Simple pleasures are often the best. You know, chocolate chip cookies and milk."

"You're right about simple pleasures being the best. Like how about a hot shower." Bryan said.

"How about a cold beer." Chet raised his bottle of Coors. They all laughed.

Carson piped up. "How about hitting a home run."

"How about sleeping ten hours after a really long day." Bryan said.

"How about a cup of hot coffee, a warm cinnamon bun and a good friend." Kate said. Then she remembered that she'd typed those very same words to Chet one lonely night last year. She looked over at him and he was squinting at her from under the rim of his baseball cap; like he was trying to figure out something. She quickly looked away.

Carson jumped up excitedly. "Hey, Dad. Look at the dolphins out there."

Chet, Cici and Bryan went over to the railing to watch the school of dolphins frolicking in the water. Kate quickly downed her glass of Chardonnay and then poured another. *God, she was losing it.*

After they had cleaned up the lunch, Kate sat on the bench and watched the others who had their lines out. Even Cici was trying her hand at fishing. Kate was feeling a little woozy and didn't trust herself to stand up.

Carson sat holding his rod. "Nothing's biting, Dad. I've been holding this forever."

"Be patient, Carson. This spot has been great lately..."

Then a minute later Carson jumped up. "Dad, I've got something. I can feel it tugging." He was giggling. Kate could see the rod bending down.

Chet came over and began to coach him through reeling in the fish. Carson was holding on for dear life, his face glowing with excitement. Chet encouraged him with clear, calm instructions. They were all cheering him on and when he brought a big fish over the side, they applauded.

"You've got yourself a nice-sized Black Fin Tuna." Chet said patting his son on the back.

Cici took Carson's picture with the fish and he glowed with pride.

Kate sat up feeling dizzy. She looked at Carson and then blurted out: 'My little boy would love to go fishing, too.'" Then her hands went to her cheeks, which had turned bright red.

Cici turned around and frowned at her. They were all looking at her. Cici said, "You have a little boy?"

"Yes, yes, I do." Kate said slowly.

"Wow! Why didn't you ever say anything before?"

"It's too painful to talk about." Kate mumbled. Then, either because of the wine or the motion of the boat or her embarrassment, she turned around and vomited over the side of the boat.

At her next session with Dr. Leah, Kate recounted the entire miserable day. "I'm so tired of keeping secrets. I can't stand much more of this."

The doctor looked at her with sympathy. "Then maybe it's time to tell the truth. Cici sounds like a sympathetic, caring individual. She'll understand."

Part 4—REDEMPTION

"There are no secrets that time does not reveal."
—Jean Racine

April-June

Chapter 45 Cici

Cici hadn't seen much of Kate this week. She'd spent several evenings with Bryan. They had made several visits with the architect to the house next to the Sunrise Café. The guy had imaginative ideas for turning the old-fashioned parlor, dining room and den into three adjoining dining areas. He suggested maintaining the quaint charm of each room and opening up the back wall onto the patio. As Bryan had planned, the Sunrise Café and the house would be joined through the kitchens, allowing for increased storage and refrigerator space for both restaurants.

Cici and Bryan spent hours going over the plans. On Friday, as they sat together on a bench in the café and looked over the drawings, Cici said, "You know, Bryan, you ought to ask Kate to take a peek at your plans. She's got a great eye for detail. I bet she'd have some ideas about decorating."

"Yeah, I've even thought about C & N Interiors. I don't know if they've ever done a restaurant."

"It wouldn't hurt to ask."

"You're so smart." Bryan bent over to kiss her on the tip of the nose, then a longer kiss on her mouth.

Pulling away, he said, "In some ways I'm more concerned about the food than the physical restaurant…I know they're both important."

"All the more reason to get some expert advice." Cici reached over and put her hand on top of Bryan's. "So what do you think was up with Kate on Sunday?"

"I think she had way too much to drink and we were sitting out in the hot sun…not a good idea."

"Right…but what about her little boy? She never mentioned having kids. I was like dumbfounded."

"She acted embarrassed when you asked about him."

"I was just shocked, is all. I'm wondering why he lives with his father and not with her. Don't they usually give kids to the mother in a divorce?"

"Give her time. One of these days she'll tell you all about it."

"Yeah, I guess."

On Sunday, Cici came home at two o'clock and found Kate paddling around in the pool. "So this is what you do while I'm hard at work," Cici said.

"Right, I just laze around. Hey, why don't you hop in and cool off?"

"I think I will. I'm going to get myself a Diet Coke with a twist of lime. Do you want one?"

"Sure, that sounds great." Kate leaned back and submerged her head in the water, letting her hair float around her.

When Cici came back in her bikini she was carrying two tall glasses of Coke. She set them down on the nearby table. Kate got out of the water and Cici plunged in. "Oh, this feels so good. Aren't we lucky to be living here?" Cici said.

"Yes, it's like a dream." Kate dried herself off with a striped bath towel, picked up her Coke and took a long drink. "This hits the spot." She spread the towel on the chaise and lay down, making happy animal sounds.

Cici giggled. "You sound like a contented brown bear." She was treading water.

"I am. I've been feeling pretty good this week." Kate sat up. "Cici, I need to talk to you about some stuff."

"Serious stuff?"

"Yeah, kind of..."

"Let's not talk about it now, okay? I just want to decompress. Things were frantic at the bakery."

"Yeah, okay. No big deal." Kate lay back down, her expression anxious.

Cici dove into the water. What was up with Kate? Maybe she wanted to talk about her little boy. Hopefully, she didn't want to move out. They got along so well.

Later, they went upstairs to change. As she pulled on some shorts, Cici yelled out to Kate. "I need to get something for my mother for her birthday. I don't have a clue what to get. She never seems to want or need anything."

Kate called back, "Let's take a trip down Duval Street and look in all the shops. Maybe you'll find something funky."

Twenty minutes later they were strolling along Duval amid a crowd of tourists. Probably a cruise ship was in town and had disgorged thousands of eager-beaver tee-shirt shoppers. They thronged the sidewalks.

Kate and Cici went in and out of shops. Cici didn't find anything that seemed quite right. As they neared Sloppy Joe's, Cici heard a voice calling her name. "Cécile, Cécile Arnaud. Over here."

Cici's heart sank. She looked up to see Myra Wilkins coming towards her. Where could she hide? She glanced over at Kate, who seemed unaware of the woman bearing down on them. Then it hit Cici—the name Cécile Arnaud didn't even register with Kate. She felt a jolt of fear. Myra was going to blow her cover.

"Hello, Cécile. I thought it was you. How are you?" Myra's eyes searched Cici's. She wore a flirty red mini-dress with spiked-heeled sandals. Next to her was a gorgeous hunk of a guy who had to be twenty years her junior. He had dark curly hair, a goatee and dark, deep-set eyes. He moved with a swagger, his black tee-shirt stretched over bulging biceps.

Cici found herself wanting to look away, hoping this wasn't happening.

Myra bent down and gave her a hug. Cici stood there like a stick figure. "We were all wondering what happened to you, Cécile," Myra said, her voice overly loud. "Harry Staples, Ben, even your buddy Jeremy didn't know where you went. Where do you live now?"

If Kate hadn't been standing right there, Cici would have lied. Instead she said, "Here, in Key West."

Myra's eyes widened. "Are you teaching?"

"No. I've got a job...a different sort of job."

"Doing what?" *God, this woman was annoying. Dr. Myra Wilkins was not her boss any more.*

"I'm working in a shop here." Cici felt Kate scrutinizing her.

"Well, we all worried so much about you after everything that happened..." Myra's words hung in the air like a big black cloud.

Cici didn't answer. She noticed that Myra hadn't introduced her gigolo, and Cici wasn't going to introduce Kate.

"So you've been able to get on with your life?"

"Yes, listen, I'm fine," Cici said in a rush. "It's nice seeing you but we're in a hurry."

Myra wouldn't let it go. Her eyes rested on Kate, with the disapproving expression Cici had seen all too often when the principal was storming around school, her minions trailing behind her. "Are you two partners? I know this is a gay community..."

Cici eyes widened and then she started to laugh. This entire encounter was way too much. "Kate, let's get going. Bye, Myra, *hasta la vista*..." Cici grabbed Kate's hand and pulled her down the sidewalk.

At the crosswalk, Cici stopped and caught her breath. "Who was that?" Kate asked, gasping for air. "And what was she talking about?

"Oh, she's someone I used to know."

171

Kate looked puzzled.

"Can you believe she thought we were two lesbians? Oh, my god." Cici grabbed Kate's arm, and they both burst out laughing. People stared, walking around them, but they couldn't stop.

"Two desperate dykes," Kate said between giggles. That started them all over again.

Cici knew her laughter verged on hysteria. It came from somewhere dark in her soul.

Chapter 46   Kate

When Kate moved from the studio apartment, she didn't give Sam her new address. She didn't want him to harass her, or worse yet, show up at her front door. She knew he flew down to Miami on business, and it would be a hop, skip and a jump to Key West. So she got a PO Box and received all her mail there.

Sam continued to send her hate mail. It was as if he wanted to control her from afar, as if he couldn't stand the fact that she wasn't under his thumb any more even though he had pushed the divorce through and then married Daniella a week later.

On the way home from work, she stopped off at the post office and checked her box. She never got much mail. Harry Stein communicated through email and she had direct deposit for her checks. Her parents' lawyer sent updates on how the probate was proceeding. Periodically, she received a couple of catalogues, but that was it.

Today, there was an envelope with Daniella's sloping handwriting. Kate recognized it from the envelope Daniella had sent with Timmy's artwork. Kate wanted to rip it open right there but decided to wait until she was home alone in her room. She put the envelope in her backpack, heavy with her laptop and drawing materials, and slung the pack over her shoulder.

As she trudged along, she thought about what Daniella might have written. Maybe there was another drawing or even a message from Timmy. He probably had begun writing in first grade.

Kate unlocked the door and Brandy came to greet her. Cici had left a note on the kitchen counter: *Out for dinner with*

Bryan. Kate figured they were spending a lot of time together since he was leaving for New York soon. Good. She was glad to be alone. She didn't know what mood she would be in after opening the letter from Daniella.

She found a knife and slit the envelope. The paper had been ripped from a notepad. The message had been scribbled using two pens, one blue and one black. The blue pen must have run out of ink. The personalized signature at the top said: *From the desk of Daniella Tripp.*

Kat,

I'm giving you a heads-up. I just can't do this mother bit much longer. We've lost another nanny. I've had to stay here babysitting the last couple of weeks. I never wanted kids and I'm feeling caged in. My career is on hold while Sam moved up to VP. It sucks. Tim is one unhappy kid. I think he needs his mother. Sam is a lousy dad. He just doesn't get kids. **Too impatient**! He's about ready to ship Tim down there. Be ready!

Daniella

Kate moved over to the sofa and sat down. She read the letter twice more. Daniella sounded strung out, definitely fed up with motherhood. Clearly, Sam and Daniella's oh-so-perfect marriage wasn't going so well.

Kate felt butterflies in her stomach. She got up to pour herself a glass of wine but after one sip she put it back on the counter. Wine wouldn't help her now. She felt thrilled and scared at the same time.

She had to talk to Cici. Last Sunday, they hadn't managed it. After they got back from their aborted shopping trip, Cici had seemed exhausted. She went up to her room and didn't even come down for dinner. During the week, Kate hadn't found the right moment to open her heart and tell Cici everything. And Cici had seemed edgy and unwilling to talk these last few days.

Kate considered the note. If Timmy came down here, he would either move in with Cici and Kate or she had to find another place for them to live. She wasn't making enough money to buy or even rent a nice two-bedroom apartment, though in August, she could expect some money from her parents' trust.

So many questions and thoughts circled in her head. How would she continue to work? Timmy would need to go to school. What would Cyril and Neil think when she dropped the bomb? She planned on telling them about her past after she talked to Cici. Then she was going to call Chet and tell him the truth. They all needed to hear the truth. Then they could decide if they wanted her friendship or not. She was exhausted from living a lie.

Chapter 47   Cici

Bryan and Cici sat at a bar in Mallory Square, drinking mojitos and sharing a plate of fried calamari while they watched the sunset. The night was perfect, soft breezes flirting with the palm trees against a brilliant orangey-pink sky.

"Would you check this over and tell me what you think?" Bryan pushed a sheet of paper over to her. "It's my letter to Reed Frost, the head chef at L'Aigle Bleu. It's one of the hottest restaurants in the Big Apple. I heard there's at least a six-month wait for a reservation. Anyway I want to meet with him while I'm in New York, maybe work in the kitchen there for a couple of weeks after I finish up my other stint. Chefs do that sometimes… let other chefs work in their kitchen to polish their skills, learn new methods."

Cici grinned. "Sure. Let me see if I've got a pen." She pushed her drink and the basket of calamari off to the side, wiped her fingers on a napkin and dug around in her purse. She fished out a pen, then spread the letter on the table and began reading. Some of the sentences were too wordy and didn't get to the point. She crossed them out, changed the order of the paragraphs and corrected the punctuation. "Hmm, I don't know if I like this last sentence." She held the pen up to her lips, deep in thought. Finally, she scratched out the sentence and added a shorter, simpler phrase. "There." She handed it back to Bryan. "Check it out and tell me what you think."

He read it slowly and then looked up. "This sounds much better. Are you sure you weren't an English teacher in your former life?" He leaned forward in his chair and considered her with a gleam in his eye.

She knew he was kidding, but her reaction took her by surprise. She blushed hotly, hands clenched in tight fists under the table. "Why do you say that?"

He was laughing, oblivious to her discomfort. "I mean, I could just see you with a red pen slashing some poor student's paper to bits."

She couldn't answer. Why didn't she just tell him the truth? She *was* an English teacher and she enjoyed picking a sentence apart and rewriting it so it flowed. As these thoughts raced through her brain, she looked up and saw Myra Wilkins threading her way to a seat on the other side of the deck. Luckily, it was almost dark now. Cici fought an irrational desire to hide under the table.

"Cici, what's up?" Bryan stared at her, his eyes narrowed. Then he turned around to see what she'd been looking at.

"Nothing, Bryan." Her voice was hard and brittle. "Just let it go."

He turned back around, looking angry. "Let what go? What in the hell is going on with you? Everything was fine a second ago and now you're pissed at me."

What Cici liked about Bryan was his easy-going personality. He was rarely ruffled but at that moment his anger was palpable across the table. But she couldn't back down, even though she knew it was wrong. "I am telling you to leave me alone. Stop quizzing me."

He glared at her. "If you're mad that I'm leaving, why don't you just say so?"

She sat there, unmoving, knowing she should apologize and stop this conversation before it raced into oblivion. "It's not that. I just don't want to talk about it."

"Cici. Talk about what? "

"Just leave me alone." She felt like a caged animal.

"Cici?" His eyes pleaded with hers. "Cici?"

She twirled the swizzle stick in her glass and watched the mint leaves swirl. "Just leave me alone, Bryan."

After what felt like an eternity, Bryan got up. He pulled out a twenty-dollar bill and tossed it on the table. "Have a nice life," he said, and walked away.

Chapter 48   Kate and Cici

Kate woke suddenly. From out of nowhere, crystal clear, she recalled the woman who'd accosted Cici on Duval Street a week ago. That day, the woman had seemed vaguely familiar. Now Kate remembered—she was the principal of Lakeland High School. Kate had seen her at a town hall meeting. The Board of Education had claimed they couldn't modernize the building because of asbestos in the walls. The principal had then presented a plan to tear down the high school and build a new one. She had spoken at length. Kate remembered needing to get home to relieve the babysitter as the woman went on and on.

What was her name? Kate couldn't remember, but she did recall the woman's outfit: a royal blue wrap dress with plenty of cleavage and super-high stiletto heels. Why had that woman accosted Cici? What had she said? Kate sat up, trying to remember. Something about teaching. Then she'd asked Cici how she'd been since 'the incident.' What incident? A sense of foreboding welled up from deep inside. Who *was* Cici? Like Kate, she didn't talk much about her past. Why not?

Heart thumping, Kate got out of bed and switched on the light. She went into the hall and paused outside Cici's door. No! First she would go downstairs. In the living room, she turned on a lamp and went into the library nook. She switched on the light over the counter. She needed lots of light.

On the lowest shelf were all of Cici's spiral notebooks. She reached up and took one down. Inside the front cover was a date. October 12th...last fall. She took down the one next to it. It was dated September 3rd. She reached up to the first notebook on the left. It was dated March of last year.

Kate started to read. Her eyes raced across the page: *I am in pain. I cannot sleep. I cannot escape what I have done. No one will ever understand how I feel. The sense of guilt, raw guilt, is overpowering. That afternoon, the snow, the wind, the cold; it haunts me. I want to die and make all this go away. Sometimes I think suicide is the only answer. Yet I am too afraid to take the razor and slice my wrists. I tried in the bathtub yesterday but I couldn't slice deep enough...*

Kate turned the page and kept reading. *I killed her. I killed a little girl. I didn't see her but it doesn't matter. I will never forgive myself...*

She closed the notebook and set it aside. Hands shaking, she pulled down another one and opened it at random. *Elisabeth Tripp, you are in my heart each and every day...*

Elisabeth? No. They'd called her Betsy. Anger bubbled up. Cici was a liar. She had lied to Kate. She was the driver of the car. She was the killer. Kate reached up and pulled down all the other notebooks. They clattered to the floor. She kicked them and stomped on them. Then she turned so fast that she hit her hand on the doorjamb. The sharp pain felt good. She ran up the stairs, turned at the landing and burst into Cici's room. The door banged against the side wall as she fumbled for the light switch. She flipped it on. The overhead fixture flooded the room with brightness.

"You did it," Kate shouted. "You killed her. You killed my baby."

Cici awoke with a jolt. At first she thought her nightmares had come to life. Kate stood by Cici's bed, her eyes blazing, her arm raised and her finger pointing. Blinded by the light and disoriented by Kate's shouting, Cici pulled her body into a ball and pressed herself against the headboard, her hands raised in front of her face.

"Answer me. You wrote pages and pages, feeling sorry for yourself. But what about Betsy? What about me? Do you feel sorry for me?" Kate spat the words, each one a blow.

Abruptly, Cici realized what was happening. *Oh, God, she's Elisabeth's mother. How could she respond to Kate, crazy with grief?* "It was an accident. I didn't mean to. I didn't see her."

"You didn't see her?" Kate moved forward, her hand raised as if ready to strike. "Was that because you were angry about losing your job? I heard about that. Were you driving like a maniac?"

"No, no. I wasn't." Cici's voice shook. "I've gone over and over that night. I couldn't see her. She was behind a snowdrift. It was a blizzard."

"What about the headlights? Couldn't you see her in the lights?" Kate was yelling.

"She was sitting on the ground. She was all dressed in white. I couldn't see anything. Just white snow."

Kate screamed—a cry from the heart, a keening from the soul. She raised her arms above her head as though beseeching the heavens.

Tears streamed down Cici's face. Kate's anguish was unbearable. Suddenly, Kate collapsed onto the floor at the foot of Cici's bed. She cradled her head on her arms, resting them on the mattress as her body shook with sobs.

Cici didn't move. She thought about how Kate had wanted to talk to her. How long had Kate known who Cici really was? Was it when they met Myra? No, she'd wanted to talk before that.

When Kate finally grew quieter, Cici took a breath and said, "I'm sorry. Kate, I'm sorry." The words hung in the air. She slid down to the foot of the bed and sat with her feet dangling over the edge. Gently, she placed her hand on Kate's head, on her black hair with the red stripe. Now she knew who Kate had been mourning all these months. "I'm sorry. Please forgive me."

Kate continued to sob. Cici slipped to the floor and sat with her back against the foot of the bed, her arms wrapped around her knees. After a long time and a last labored sob, Kate turned and sat next to Cici in a similar pose.

"It was really my fault," Kate said. Her voice was low and robotic, as though she was repeating a memorized lesson. "I was upstairs on the internet. I thought she was downstairs with Timmy, watching *Curious George*. I'd put up the fence but she climbed over it." Kate voice trembled. "Then she put on Timmy's boots. They were much too big. And she put on her hat and mittens. But not her coat. She couldn't reach it. She went out the front door. I hadn't put on the safety bolt and she figured out how to open it. I was a bad mother. I've relived that night over and over…every day…I can't escape what I did."

Cici thought through everything that had happened this past year. In some ways, she and Kate had been mirror images of each other, each tortured by a single moment in their lives.

They sat there together on the floor without talking. Finally Cici sighed and said, "Let's go downstairs and make coffee. We're not going back to sleep."

Chapter 49 Cici

They sat together at the dining table and talked. There was so much to say now that they weren't treading through a minefield of secrets. "Why did you ever marry Sam?" Cici asked. "It sounds like he was a jerk from the get-go."

"I think I was trying to do what my parents wanted. I had never lived away from home and was always the dutiful daughter. My dad loved Sam, especially on the football field. He had no idea what Sam was really like."

"What about later?"

"Once he was out of college and we'd moved away, Sam didn't want anything to do with my parents. I think at that point they began to wonder about our marriage, but they didn't ask me about it much or try to help. I'm not sure they even knew what to do. I felt too ashamed to tell them how bad it was."

Cici got up to refill their mugs. When she sat back down, Kate told her about Daniella and the divorce. "After the accident, Sam convinced me I was to blame for Betsy's death. I was irrational, drowning in grief, and I believed everything he said. He always had terrific power over me. I spent three months locked in the bedroom while he put through the divorce papers. I signed every document and gave him full custody of Timmy. In the end, he gave me a thousand dollars and kicked me out of the house."

Cici clasped her mug in her hands. "Where did you go?"

"I went to live in my parents' empty house. My dad had died the previous year. My mother was in an Alzheimer's nursing home. It was a weird time. I can barely remember those days. I visited my mom and worked in the garden. After

183

only a couple of months, my mother died and I was totally alone."

"Oh, my God. You've been through hell." Cici reached across the table. Kate took her hand and held on tight.

"Tell me about Betsy," Cici said. "I want to know everything about her."

Kate's face lit up. "She always knew exactly what she wanted. That's what I loved most about her. Sometimes she was a lot to handle. Oh, boy, we did have our battles." Kate laughed. "But she could also be incredibly sweet." Tears filled her eyes. Cici nodded her eyes moist as well.

"But what's really scary now is I can barely remember what she looked like. All I have is the picture in my locket." She got up, came around to Cici's side of the table and opened up the silver heart.

Cici smiled. "Oh, she's adorable. Now I can see how much she looks like you."

"What do you mean?"

Cici stood and went into the library alcove. She pulled a chair over, climbed on it and reached for a file folder on the top shelf. She hopped down, came back to the dining table and handed the file to Kate.

Kate laid the file on the table and opened it. Inside were clippings from the *Lakeland Times* and the *Chicago Tribune*. They recounted the story of the accident and included several pictures of Betsy. Kate leafed through the clippings, gazing at the pictures. In one, the little girl wore a pink sun hat and was frowning. Another picture showed Betsy giggling at the door of a play house. Tears ran down Kate's cheeks as she ran one finger down Betsy's chubby cheek.

"If you want those, they're yours," Cici said quietly.

Kate looked up, overcome. "Oh, Cici, this is the most wonderful present in the world."

They fell silent.

Then Kate looked up, her tear-streaked cheeks pink and her expression anxious. "There's something else I need to talk to you about." She closed the file, reached for her coffee mug and took a sip. "I need to ask your permission, I guess."

Cici sat up straight, elbows on the table. "Permission?"

"I got a letter a few days ago from Daniella, Sam's wife."

"Yes."

Kate bent forward, cupping her mug in her hands. "Daniella thinks Sam is going to send Timmy down here to me. It sounds like they're fed up with taking care of him." Her fingers tightened around the mug. She smiled uncertainly at Cici. "And, well, he would have to come here."

"To live with us?"

"Yes, until I can find somewhere else to live. I'll be able to do that sometime this summer after probate on my mother's will is finished and I have some cash."

"Of course he can come here, Kate. Don't worry. It'll be fun." Cici bent down and patted Brandy, who was sprawled out under the table. "Brandy, you're going to have company; somebody to throw your ball." Then she looked up. "Hey, we can fix up the attic room. Make it a third bedroom. Maybe we can get Cyril to help?"

Kate got up and came around the table. She wrapped Cici in a fierce hug. "I'm sorry about earlier. I'm sorry for what I said. I went crazy," Kate said.

Cici hugged back, too overwhelmed to say a word.

Together they put away the notebooks scattered across the alcove, then went into the kitchen and made bacon and eggs. As they worked Cici described the terrible weeks after the accident. "I changed my name when I came down here," She said as she laid bacon in a pan. "I felt so guilty. I didn't want anyone to find me."

Kate gave her a wan smile. "That's why I went back to my maiden name...so I could hide out."

They ate their early breakfast, and Cici glanced at the clock. "I'm going to call Bryan. He's usually up at four. We need to talk." She bit her lip. "We had an argument last night. I want to set things straight. I'm tired of lying." She looked at Kate. "Do you mind if I tell him everything?"

"No. I think it's important for both of us to talk to our friends. Dr. Leah, my shrink, told me I needed to unburden myself to find peace. She was right."

"The truth sets you free," Cici murmured.

Kate got up to clear the table. With her back to Cici, she rinsed the plates. Then she stood there, not turning around. "Cici?"

"Yeah?" Cici folded up the placemats to put them in the kitchen drawer.

Kate turned around and met Cici's eyes. "I have to talk to Chet."

"Chet? I didn't think you even liked him. You've been so, I don't know, standoffish around him."

Kate took a deep breath. "Chet and I chatted online for a year and a half. I know him really well."

Cici stared. "You've got to be kidding."

Kate's pale cheeks were turning bright pink. "I met him on a matchmaker site. We talked to each other about everything. I knew all about Carson and he knew all about my kids and my unhappy marriage. I always felt guilty about our relationship, but I got so lonely..." She swallowed. "After the accident, I never talked to him again. But now...I think I need to."

Chapter 50   Cici and Bryan

"Hello?" Bryan sounded groggy on the other end of the phone.

"Hi, It's me."

"Cici? It's four o'clock."

"I know. I need to talk to you."

"Now?"

"Please, Bryan. I need to explain everything."

"I've got to get to the café. I don't know if this is a good idea."

"It is. I'll meet you at the café at four-thirty."

He was silent for a few seconds. "No, I'll pick you up in ten minutes. I don't think you should be out walking alone at this hour."

Cici smiled. "I'll be ready."

. She hung up, then ran up the stairs. She could hear Kate in the shower, singing. That was a first. Cici splashed water on her face, brushed her teeth and ran a comb through her hair. In her bedroom, she took off her nightgown and pulled on some jean shorts, a white tee-shirt and a red hooded sweatshirt. Her flip flops were downstairs by the door. When Bryan's truck came down the street she was out the door and down the steps.

At the curb Bryan reached over and pushed open the passenger door. He said hi without looking at her. They didn't talk on the way to the Sunrise Café. Cici didn't want to say anything until they were face to face with no distractions. At the stop light, in the red glow, she could feel Bryan's gaze on her.

Bryan drove around to the side of the café. They both got out and walked to the back door. He keyed in the code and she followed him down the short hall to the kitchen.

187

He switched on the lights. "I'll make coffee."

"I probably don't need any. I already drank a gallon this morning." She sounded unnaturally bright and chirpy.

"Well, I'm making a pot. You do what you want." He wasn't ready to warm up to her yet. While the coffee brewed, Bryan turned on the ovens, went into the dining room and turned on the lights there.

A knock came at the back door. A delivery man rolled in cartons of milk, cream, butter and eggs. He and Bryan laughed about something. Bryan didn't introduce her. After he left, Cici helped Bryan stash things in the walk-in refrigerator. They didn't talk.

Bryan poured himself a cup of coffee and put in cream and sugar. "You're sure you don't want any coffee?"

"Okay, I'll have some with you." She smiled brightly.

He poured her a cup and added cream and sugar just like his own. Cici didn't say anything He sat on a metal stool on one side of the stainless steel table and she sat on the other side. He pushed the coffee over to her. "So?" he said, finally looking at her, his eyes wary.

"Bryan, I've been keeping secrets. I want to tell you what happened a year ago and what happened this morning at two AM."

Bryan held his own mug in both hands and gazed at her over the rim. She couldn't tell anything from his expression, except that he wasn't going to make this easy.

She began by telling him about Lakeland High School. When she got to that last day, and the accident, her eyes filled with tears but she kept going. Bryan's face reflected her pain and anguish. He reached out as if to take her hand but she slipped it down onto her lap. Then she told him about the months living at her mother's bakery, working with Oscar, and then Oscar's offer of the house in Key West. Her narrative flowed like a practiced storyteller's. But of course it did, she'd

188

been repeating this story in her head and in her notebooks for days and weeks and months.

At first, Bryan could hardly believe what he was hearing. He sat there, his coffee untouched, and simply absorbed what Cici was telling him. Finally, she stopped talking. She sat before him, so delicate-looking with the pixie haircut, her eyes luminous, her lips in a soft natural pout. The red hoodie stood up around her neck like Queen Elizabeth's lace collar.

"I've been hiding what happened; who I really am," she said. "I've been wallowing in guilt for over a year. That's what last night was about; why I snapped at you and told you to leave me alone. I was actually petrified because I saw my former principal across from us and I didn't want you to learn who I really was." Cici looked at him, her eyes pleading for forgiveness.

He got up and went to her, pulled her up from the stool and held her close. Then he sat down, holding her on his lap. She nestled against his chest, her head under his chin. "Cici, you could have told me all this ages ago. I would have understood. Don't you know that?" He turned her face up to his and kissed her tenderly.

They were quiet for a moment and then she said, "I haven't finished. The child I killed was named Betsy Tripp. Guess who her mother is?"

Bryan raised his eyebrows. "No clue."

"It's Kate. She came down to Key West to escape, just like me."

He shook his head in disbelief. "Unbelievable. This is like some crazy soap opera."

Another knock at the door roused them. Bryan got up and went down the hall. He came back with Napoléon, both of

189

them carrying boxes of croissants and bread from the Guérin Bakery.

"What are you doing here, Mademoiselle Cécile?" Napoléon asked.

"Just conspiring with Bryan and having morning coffee." Cici looked at her watch. "Oh, my God, I better get going. I've only got twenty minutes before I'm supposed to be at the bakery. Napoléon, could you drop me off at home while you're on your rounds?"

"*Bien sûr, pas de problème.*"

Cici reached up and kissed Bryan goodbye. "See you later."

Chapter 51   Kate

4 AM – Hello. It's me. Is this still your email address? I apologize for disappearing so suddenly with no explanation. I've been through a lot. I'm divorced and I've moved to a new town. Red Queen

7 AM – Hello. I was surprised to see your message this morning. You must have been up early. I wondered what had happened to you since last year…   Deep Sea Sailor

7:05 AM – There's a lot to tell you. I wondered if you wanted to reconnect or just move on?   Red Queen

7:10 AM – I need to get Carson ready for school. Let me think about all this. I'll connect with you tonight after 8:30. Deep Sea Sailor

8:45 PM – We read three stories tonight. Carson reads one page and I read the next. It's time consuming but his reading has really improved and I enjoy doing it. How are your kids? I hope they're doing well. I've been thinking about reconnecting off and on all day. I don't know if it's a good idea. It sounds as though you've moved on… Deep Sea Sailor

8:50 PM – A year ago, I was somebody's doormat. Now I want to stand on my own two feet. But that doesn't mean I don't want to chat. We used to have such good talks. Red Queen

8:55 PM – You want to just start up where we left off? I don't know. After you "left" I realized I depended on those conversations. I'm wondering if I want to start up again. Deep Sea Sailor

9:00 PM – I understand how you feel. It wasn't about you. For a year, I never went online. I didn't even own a

191

computer. I was emotionally destroyed and couldn't relate to anyone. Red Queen

    9:02 PM – What happened? Deep Sea Sailor

    9:03 PM – I'd rather tell you in person. Could you meet me at the Southernmost Beach Café tomorrow evening? Red Queen

    9:04 PM – Here? Key West? Tomorrow? Deep Sea Sailor

    9:05 PM – Yes. I'm here. Red Queen

    9:07 PM – What is this, some kind of joke? How long have you been here? Deep Sea Sailor

    9:08 PM – A while… Red Queen

    9:09 PM – That's a cryptic answer. Maybe this is a bad idea. Deep Sea Sailor

    9:10 PM – Please, just meet me and I'll explain everything. Can anyone take care of Carson for an hour? Red Queen

    9:30 PM – Carson is going over to my parents' house for dinner. I can meet you at 7:00 PM at the Café. Deep Sea Sailor

    9:31 PM – Thank you. Red Queen

    9:32 PM – How will I know you? Deep Sea Sailor

    9:33 PM – You'll know me as soon as you see me. Red Queen

Chapter 52   Chet

At seven on the dot, Chet walked into the restaurant. He checked out the bar and the inside dining room, but saw no single women. He stepped out onto the patio and looked around. The Southernmost Beach Café was right on the sand, a perfect spot to enjoy the light breeze off the water. Only a few vacationers were left on the beach as the sun began its descent.

Since it was a warm night, several people were having dinner outside. Over in the corner, he recognized Cici's roommate Kate. She must be meeting someone for dinner. She was gazing out over the water and didn't look his way. He debated whether to go over and say hello, but decided against it. She'd acted so strange that day on his boat, and always seemed distant the few times they'd met.

He stepped back inside the restaurant and looked around again. Then he went to the bar to wait for The Red Queen. Maybe she was late. Maybe she wasn't coming. Maybe it was all a hoax? He wondered if a techy whiz could hack into the matchmaking site and impersonate someone.

When the barman asked him what he wanted, he ordered a beer. He stood there drinking it and ate a handful of peanuts. The place was getting busy.

A little while later he checked his watch. Seven-twenty and still no sign of anyone likely to be her. You'll know me, she'd said. What did that mean? Irritated, he wondered how long he should wait. He felt as though he'd been conned.

He paid the bartender and drained his glass. Then he went back out for a last look at the patio. Maybe she'd come up along the beachfront. He still saw no single women who looked like they were waiting for anyone. Except Kate, who spotted him and waved. He suppressed a sigh, knowing he'd have to go over there and say hello.

As he approached the table, she stood up. Her short emerald green dress showed off her perfect body, and he had to admit she was a beautiful woman. Too bad she had zero personality.

"Chet?" She was looking right at him. She'd always avoided his eyes before.

"Hello, Kate."

She held out her hand, smiling, a glow in her eyes. "It's me."

Out of politeness, he took it. Her slim hand felt warm in his. "Yeah, hi," he said, not sure how to take her odd remark. "I came here to meet someone. But they didn't show, so I guess I won't stick around." He slipped his hand from her grasp and started to turn away.

"It's me," she repeated.

He frowned.

"I'm the Red Queen."

He stared at her. She was the Red Queen? She didn't exactly match her online picture. "What about the red hair?" He'd loved the red hair.

"I dyed it black… for many reasons." She flattened her hair and bent her head. Beneath the black color he could see an inch of red roots.

He felt unnerved, unsure how to deal with this woman who'd seemed like an ice queen instead of his friendly online muse. "I'm afraid I don't recognize you."

She laughed. "I think I weighed about twenty pounds more then."

He backtracked. "I didn't mean you're not attractive now, actually you're beautiful…but the girl I knew, she was beautiful too."

"That girl was me, Chet. And thanks for the compliment. You're pretty handsome yourself."

Chet blushed. "Let's sit down and talk," Kate said.

After they both were seated, the waiter came over. Kate ordered a glass of tonic water with lime and Chet got another beer. They put the menus aside, more interested in talk than food.

"I owe you an explanation," she said. "There's so much to tell. For a period of time, I didn't feel worthy of your friendship. I broke off from everyone I knew and hovered on the brink of suicide." She bit her lip and gazed at him, her eyes glazed with unshed tears. "Let me tell you what happened and you can judge whether you want to step back into my life."

Over the next hour, she told him about her daughter. The snowstorm, the accident and Betsy's death. They ordered something for dinner in the midst of this, but Kate left hers untouched, and afterward Chet could barely recall what he'd eaten.

In her eyes he glimpsed the depth of her pain. She held a Kleenex and every so often dabbed away tears as one emotion after another swept across her face: grief, regret, sometimes anger. She spoke of her divorce, Sam kicking her out of her home and taking custody of their son. Chet wondered how he would feel if something happened to Carson. Would he react similarly, or would he be able to forgive? The death of a child could easily destroy a marriage.

Kate talked about coming down to Key West. "I think ultimately I wanted to reach out to you. You'd been a mainstay in my life. What did I have? My beautiful children and conversations with you. But when Betsy died, I blamed the time I spent on the computer. If I hadn't been upstairs working, I would have heard her go outside. I also blamed the time I spent with you...which was often my salvation. Do you see?" Her face was an open canvas, devoid of guile. Clearly she wanted him to understand.

Chet said, "When you stopped emailing me, I was disappointed…no, unhappy…and then angry. I'm embarrassed how much I depended on sharing my day with you. You were always my best listener about Carson, the business and, well, other stuff." He shook his head. "I just couldn't get over it. My wife left us high and dry, and your disappearance was another rejection. I kept wondering what had happened; if I'd said something wrong; if your marriage had improved; if you had died…" He turned and looked out at the ocean. The waves pounded rhythmically against the shoreline. He loved the ocean. To him it represented the power and constancy of Nature. All the time he and Kate had been going through this emotional trauma, the waves kept thundering in on the beach.

"I'm sorry," Kate said as he turned back to look at her.

He reached out and grasped her hand. Touching her was a new experience. He looked at their entwined fingers. "This is so bizarre. An online romance depends on the written word. Now I can see your face, feel your hand in mine, hear your voice. I feel like I'm meeting someone new. Do you know what I mean?"

"Yes. Yes, I do."

They fell silent. Then Kate said, "I haven't told you everything." She spoke about Dr. Zuckerman and how helpful she had been. Then she said, "Do you know who was driving the car that accidentally hit Betsy?"

Chet shook his head.

"Cici was. She moved down here to start a new life. Like me, she went through hell after the accident, blaming herself. We discovered our connection yesterday morning. Just like me, she thought she could escape the past…but you can't. So now we're going to face it together."

Chapter 53   Cici and Kate

This was the long-awaited day. Kate and Cici were driving up Highway A1A to Miami, going to the airport to pick up Timothy Tripp. Cici drove Bryan's Ford convertible with the top down. The wind ruffled their hair and they felt on top of the world.

Several weeks earlier, Bryan had convinced Cici to get back in the driver's seat. She was reluctant at first, but after driving with him around town, she began to feel more comfortable behind the wheel. When he left for New York, he gave her the keys to the Ford and the truck. "I'll be visiting Tiffany's when I'm in New York," he'd said, with a meaningful look when he kissed her goodbye. Would that mean a silver chain or a diamond ring? Her heart skipped a beat when she thought about it.

She glanced over at Kate. "This is your big day. Aren't you excited?"

"Yes. In so many ways this seems like a new beginning, you know what I mean?"

"I do." Cici watched a car pass them on the left.

"I still can't believe Daniella left Sam. She did what I should've done." A cynical look crossed her face. "He could hardly wait to wash his hands of Timmy the minute he had to be a solo parent. You should have heard him on the phone. Arrogant, yelling… giving orders.. I shudder to think what Timmy's life has been like this past year. He's going to need a lot of help."

"What did Dr. Leah say?"

"She gave me the names of a couple of therapists. They're both really great with children."

They fell silent briefly, content to enjoy the drive and the breeze. Then Cici said, "So Kate, we haven't talked much about Chet and you. What did he say when you told him?"

Kate reached up and fluffed her short red hair. Zanzibar had cut and styled it the day before. She felt exposed with her neck and face bare. The long, black hair that had hung around her face and shoulders had been a kind of mask she could hide behind. Now her face was open to the world. "I think Chet still doesn't know what to make of me. I mean, he understands what happened, but he doesn't recognize me as the person he used to chat with online. Does that make sense? I guess, in his mind, I was a different person." She paused, thinking. "I probably was. We've decided to get together to do stuff with the kids. We're both hoping Timmy and Carson will get along." She turned to face Cici. "We're going to take it slow...try to get to know each other with no strings attached."

"Is that good for you?"

"Yes. I'm just becoming my own person. I don't think I'm ready to jump into a wild romance." She smiled at Cici.

They drove along with glimpses of the Atlantic and the Gulf on each side of the thin strip of land. Seagulls swooped through the sky and sandpipers ran across the sandy beaches.

"I've been thinking about the guilt we both felt." Cici spoke slowly and thoughtfully. "It's a self-centered, egotistical emotion, you know? Wallowing in all that remorse did nothing, achieved nothing, and made me miserable." She gripped the steering wheel harder as she talked.

Kate was staring ahead, her face unguarded and vulnerable.

"What I realized is, rather than, *why me*? I should be thinking *what now? Why me, why did this happen* keeps you frozen in place. With *what now*, I have to move ahead. Do something. Make a change."

198

Kate clenched her hands in her lap and then opened them, palms up. "You're right. It's not about *why me, why poor me*, it's about, *what's next, where do I go from here*." She reached over and lightly touched Cici's bare arm. "What an insight. You're so right."

Cici banged on the steering wheel, making the horn blast. "Today is the future." She proclaimed. They both laughed.

In Islamorada, they stopped for key lime ice cream cones at Mr. C's. Back on the road, Cici turned up the radio. They drove down the highway with the music blasting, singing along and laughing.

When *Brave* by Sara Bareilles came on, Cici said, "Oh my God, I love this song." She grinned at Kate. "This is our song." They sang along, voices loud in the breezy sunshine:

> *Maybe there's a way out of the cage where you live*
> *Maybe one of these days you can let the light in*
> *Show me how big your brave is...*
> *And since your history of silence*
> *Won't do you any good,*
> *Did you think it would?*
> *Let your words be anything but empty.*
> *Why don't you tell them the truth?*
> *Say what you wanna say*
> *And let the words fall out*
> *Honestly I wanna see you be brave...*

Made in the USA
Columbia, SC
07 May 2022

59766879R00113